Colt Granger walked in carrying his hat in his hands.

His sun-kissed hair surrounded that beautiful face of his. His crystal-blue eyes sparkled as a sheepish grin spread across his kissable lips. The man looked sexier than a cowboy had a right to. Helen desperately wished she'd worn something less comfortable. She tried to straighten out the collar on her pajamas.

"I wasn't expecting company."

"You look beautiful," he said.

Sincerity crossed his face, making her uncomfortable.

There's room on this sofa if you want to join me."

I'd be happy to."

Colt sat on the opposite end of the couch. Helen was dying to ask him all sorts of questions about how he was feeling about her news. She wanted to tell him she understood that her announcement must have come as a complete shock to him.

But most of all, she wanted to let him know she forgave him for walking away.

She wanted to share all of these things with him and more.

Dear Reader,

What a joy it is to be writing about the Grangers and Briggs, Idaho. Each story seems to capture my imagination more than I ever thought possible, and this one is no exception. In researching this book, I learned some intriguing information about Cowboy Mounted Shooting that I hope you'll find as captivating as I did. It's one heck of a sport.

Once again, I attended the Zane Gray's West Society conference that took place in Provo, Utah. This time we were lucky to have a handful of Zane Gray's movies available for viewing. What a delight to be able to enjoy a traditional, 1940s Western on the big screen, where cowboy values reigned supreme. Some of the heroes in the movies reminded me of Colt Granger, the hero in this book. I crafted his character to represent both historic cowboy values along with a more modern take on cowboy ethos. Not only does Colt have to solve a land issue and learn how to corral his three rowdy sons, but he has to win the heart of a self-reliant cowgirl named Helen Shaw, who's more comfortable on the back of a horse than she ever could be with a baby in her arms.

You can visit me at www.maryleo.com, where you'll find some fun facts about old-time cowboys, Idaho's Teton Valley and my favorite Christmas cookie recipes. You can also find me on Facebook, where I'll keep you informed of my latest books.

Best,

Mary Leo

AIMING FOR THE COWBOY

MARY LEO

⊕ HARLEQUIN® AMERICAN ROMANCE®

Recycling programs
for this product may
not exist in your area.

ISBN-13: 978-0-373-75512-7

AIMING FOR THE COWBOY

Printed in U.S.A.

ABOUT THE AUTHOR

Mary Leo grew up in South Chicago in the tangle of a big Italian family. She's worked in Hollywood, Las Vegas and in Silicon Valley. Currently she lives in San Diego with her husband, author Terry Watkins, and their sweet kitty, Sophie.

Books by Mary Leo

HARLEQUIN AMERICAN ROMANCE
1423—FALLING FOR THE COWBOY

For Indie-Elise, the absolute sweetest grandbaby I could ever hope for. And to her loving and dedicated parents, Jocelyn and Paul, who are simply the best mom and dad ever!

Chapter One

The hoots and whistles from the crowd in the stands at Horsemen's Arena in Las Vegas should have been enough to give Helen Shaw the adrenaline rush she needed to jack up her excitement for the coming event. But it wasn't.

As she and her horse, Tater—a honey-colored Nokota she had purchased from Colt Granger two years ago— made their way out to the main arena, Helen's stomach brutally pitched, reminding her that something was definitely off this evening.

"Shoot 'em dead," her teammate Sarah Hunter yelled as Helen passed her. Sarah's ride would be coming up after two more riders competed.

"You, too!" Helen yelled back to her. They were on the same team, but they competed individually, which was the reason why Helen liked the sport so much. Even though they were competitors, everyone in the equine sport acted as if they were all part of one big extended family, which was something Helen needed at the moment, a friendly reminder that she would be all right.

Instead of focusing in on her game, Helen was busy gulping down deep breaths of rich animal-scented air, trying to calm her overactive stomach. The familiar smells of horse stalls usually quieted any nerves she might have, so she didn't understand the growing nausea.

What could she have eaten to cause such a reaction in her stomach? Yes, she was nervous, but she'd checked and rechecked everything: the braided rein felt steady in her hands; her two single-shot Cimarron .45s were loaded with black powder and secure in their double front rig; her royal-blue cattleman-type hat sat snug on her head; the custom-made, matching blue leather chaps hung easy on her legs; and the lapis lazuli flower pendant her friend Colt had given her for good luck felt a little like his warm kisses around her neck.

She was ready to take on this moment. If she won, she would move on to the next regional championship event for cowboy mounted shooting in the fall. Something she'd been working toward for the past three years.

Tater slowed to an easy canter as they made their way through the metal gate. Helen could hear the *pop-pop-pop* from the male competitor in front of her as he fired at the target balloons from his mount. An announcer rattled on about the cowboy's time and his abilities in the usual jumble of garbled words that large arenas' PA systems seemed to produce.

Then, in an instant, the crowd whistled and cheered as Helen and the cowboy passed each other, nodding recognition as she and Tater finally reached their starting point.

The announcer mumbled something about Tater then focused on there being a lady in the house, which he did every time a woman rode out. Cowboy mounted shooting was one of the few events where women and men competed against each other, and because of this, most of the announcers seemed to overcompensate with political correctness to let the audience know a "lady" had approached the main arena.

Helen eased Tater into a faster canter, making tight circles in front of the short course. The buzzer sounded and without much thought, Helen drew her first weapon, leaned forward in the saddle, and Tater took off for the semicircle of five white balloons. In one swift movement Helen took aim, clicked back the rough hammer, pulled the trigger and popped the first balloon, then the second, third, fourth and fifth. She quickly holstered her gun and drew the second firearm, all the while guiding Tater around the red barrel at the far end of the course, his hooves pounding dirt, his breathing hard and heavy. Tater felt like the wind guiding her toward each target. The constant hammering of his strong legs and the sharp angle of his muscled body as they rounded the barrel added to Helen's supreme confidence and focus. She took aim once again and popped each of the five remaining red balloons on the run down as she and Tater raced straight to the end of the course. Holstering her second gun, totally in sync with her horse, totally in tune with the power of the event, Helen knew she'd broken a record.

The crowd cheered. The announcer did his "woo-hoo" bit, and continued his warble about how "this cowgirl can ride!" Then he gave the audience her overall ranking stats as everyone waited for her score.

When the clatter died down, Helen and Tater eased up to a more effortless gait, and she noticed the five-foot-tall digital clock gave her a winning time.

"We did it, boy."

Helen beamed, and just as she patted her approval on Tater's hindquarters, the nausea overtook her with a vengeance. This time Helen couldn't control it and she vomited down the side of her lovely blue chaps, causing what could only be described as an overreaction by the handlers, who immediately called in medical.

Suspecting the flu, her team leader insisted she see a doctor, and before Helen could get herself together enough to object to all the fuss, she was transported to an urgent care facility, where an overly sympathetic nurse and stoic female doctor hit her with a barrage of questions. When Helen admitted this wasn't the first time she'd vomited in the past few weeks, the doctor recommended a complete physical, which included a urine sample and enough vials of blood to satisfy a vampire.

"The good news is you don't have the flu," Doctor Joyce said as she slipped off her latex gloves and tossed them in the small silver trash can. "You can sit up."

Helen slid her feet out of the stirrups and quickly pushed herself upright, holding the front of her paper gown closed, ready for anything the doctor threw at her.

"That sounds as if there's some bad news coming. Give it to me straight, Doc. I can handle it." Helen let out a heavy sigh as anxiety gripped her body. She'd been feeling sick for weeks, and suspected the absolute worse, but was hoping it would pass.

It hadn't.

She knew all about cancer and heart disease, both of which had claimed the lives of several family members. She only hoped if it was something horrible, she had time to do a few of the things on her bucket list.

She sighed. "How much time do I have?"

"About seven months," Doctor Joyce told her in a calm voice.

Helen figured that's how these things went. The doctor remained composed while the patient freaked out.

Helen was not the freak-out type. She prided herself on remaining cool under any circumstance. "Will I suffer?"

"That depends."

Despite her strong inner convictions, Helen's eyes welled up as hot tears stung her face. She wiped them away with the tissue Doctor Joyce offered her. "I always knew it would be like this, but I thought I'd have more time. There's so much I want to do. So many things I want to see. But mostly, I want to win the world championship of cowboy mounted shooting. I'm so close I can taste it."

Doctor Joyce wrote something down in Helen's file then sat on a black stool. "You'll still get to do those things, just not this year. You can even ride until the baby makes you feel unbalanced, if you take it easy."

Helen stopped crying, hiccuped and drew in a rough breath. "Baby? What do babies have to do with the fact that I'm dying?"

"Whatever gave you that idea?"

"You said I have only months to live."

Doctor Joyce chuckled, at least Helen thought it was a chuckle. Her somber expression never completely changed. "You can look at it that way if you want to, but that's not what I meant. You're pregnant and your baby is due in about seven months. Because you're not sure of the date of your last period, you'll need an ultrasound to get a more accurate date. Your gynecologist at home can order that, but from my initial exam, you're approximately seven to eight weeks pregnant."

Acid swirled inside Helen's stomach. Her chest tightened. Her hands felt clammy. If she wasn't half-naked, she'd run out of the tiny office screaming. "Pregnant! Me? No. Not possible. It must be a tumor or a deadly wart."

"Trust me. It's a fetus."

"You don't understand. That's completely impossible."

"If you have intercourse with a man, it's *completely* possible."

Helen drew in a deep, calming breath. The doctor had to be wrong. Everyone knew Vegas doctors were less than great, and this one was just plain dumb.

"He's had a vasectomy," Helen spit out.

"It's rare, but there's a one percent chance of pregnancy during the first five years after a vasectomy."

"So it can't happen."

"It already did."

"But we only had sex one time. We're friends, not lovers. Colt won't want—" She stopped talking. News traveled like a wildfire during these championships. "Who else knows about this?"

"You, me and soon your team leader."

"You can't tell anyone."

"He'll want to know if you're fit to ride, which you are not. At least not in competition."

Helen didn't want to dwell on that last statement at the moment. She had other, more pressing concerns. "Can't you make up something? I don't want anyone to know I'm—" The word caught in her throat.

"Pregnant?"

Helen nodded, desperately trying to come to terms with the whole idea of having an actual baby growing inside her. An actual child. A dependent. A munchkin she never thought would come out of her body. Babies were for her friends, her relatives, people who wanted to reproduce.

She wasn't one of them.

"If that's how you want it, I won't tell anyone, but

you shouldn't ride competitively while you're pregnant. If you're thrown, you could lose the baby."

"I've never been thrown from a horse, and I've been riding for over twenty years."

"It's a precaution. In the meantime, eat ginger for your nausea, get plenty of rest and increase your calorie intake. You might want to consider eating smaller meals. Sometimes that helps. Start taking prenatal vitamins— you can get them just about anywhere—and try to add plenty of calcium to your diet. Make an appointment with an ob-gyn when you get home."

"This is happening too fast. It changes everything. I don't like change. It throws off my equilibrium."

The doctor hesitated for a beat. "There are other options if you don't want this baby."

Her words hit Helen like a shock wave, taking her breath away.

When she was able to breathe again, she protested, "Who said anything about options? Of course I want this baby. I'd be crazy not to…wouldn't I?" She paused as the thought of other options settled in her mind.

She shook her head. "I'm pregnant, and I'm staying that way, at least for the next seven months anyway." Her heart skipped a beat. "I'm pregnant!"

The enormity of her condition began to sink in. The idea of motherhood scared her silly. Yes, she loved kids, as long as they belonged to someone else, and yes, she sometimes liked Colt's boys, when they weren't dropping frogs in her drink or using the latticework in her backyard as target practice with her spring fruit. She didn't have to discipline them or worry if they were eating their veggies or tormenting their teachers. But most of all, she didn't have to be responsible for anyone but herself.

She'd always prided herself on her freedom. Her independence. She could join the rodeo circuit and be gone for months at a time. Pursue her dreams. Be a free spirit. Make love with no strings attached.

Suddenly that flimsy string had turned into a rope, a thick rope that tied her to Colt Granger, a rope made out of ten-gauge steel that could never be cut.

Never, no matter what.

She shivered at the thought, or was it simply cold in the office? Truth be told, she didn't know much of anything at the moment. Her brain was in a state of shock. Thinking was not part of its current function.

"Great. Then congratulations, Helen Shaw. You're going to be a mom." A warm smile spread across the doctor's face as a tsunami of nausea drenched Helen in warm sweat.

"I'm glad somebody thinks so," Helen mumbled while trying to get control over her roiling stomach.

Now all she had to do was figure out a way to tell Colt, a man who most certainly did not want another child. A man who could barely handle the kids he already had, let alone one more. A man she'd tried her best to steer clear of, knowing full well he represented everything she didn't want. She had known better not to sleep with him.

They were merely friends.

Nothing more.

But she'd done it anyway.

Now what?

"Cheer up. At least you're not dying," the doctor said on her way out the door.

Helen nodded, smiled and decided dying might have been the better option.

And as if the universe was angry at her for thinking such a horrible thought, nausea overtook her and she vomited in the tiny trash can right on top of Doctor Joyce's latex gloves.

FOUR-YEAR-OLD JOEY GRANGER sat up on the edge of the red slate roof of the two-story barn swinging his legs, looking as happy as a fly on a honey pie. It was his birthday, and Dodge, his gramps, had invited half the town of Briggs, Idaho, for the annual spring barbecue on the Granger family ranch, a sprawling homestead that encompassed enough land for a sizable commercial potato crop, a hundred head of cattle, three ranch houses, a couple stables, several outbuildings and enough open range for deer and elk to call it home. The ranch landscape included grassy hills and valleys, acres of flat land and an assortment of towering trees. Dodge lived in the main house, along with Colt's brother Doc Blake, a pediatric dentist who had transformed half of the house into his dental office, his young daughter, Scout, and his wife, Maggie. The house had a view of the Teton mountain range to the east, and a sky that wouldn't quit to the west.

Travis, the youngest of the three brothers, had built his own house as soon as he was old enough to live on his own on the northeast corner of the land, closer to the town of Briggs itself, about a fifteen minute drive from the main house. Then there was Colt's place, which he built on a bend in the Snake River, which ran through the property. Colt figured it to be the perfect location for raising three spirited boys, Joey being his youngest.

Unfortunately for Colt, most of the townsfolk and their kids had decided to attend the birthday celebration, including Jenny Pickens, Colt's latest match-up courtesy of his brother Travis, who had assured him this girl would be the perfect fit. A fine gesture if he was at all interested in another woman, but ever since he'd slept with Helen Shaw the search had come to a grinding halt. Problem was he knew darn well that capturing Helen's heart seemed as probable as his trying to catch a raindrop in a thunderstorm. The girl had already planned out her life, and it didn't include raising three strong-willed boys on a potato ranch in Briggs, Idaho.

Still, he couldn't stop thinking about her.

The heck if he hadn't struggled to get her out of his head. But she lingered on him like the scent of cherry blossoms in spring. It should never have happened. They were good friends and he had aimed to keep it that way, hadn't meant for it to go any further, never planned to take the friendship to the bedroom. But he'd given her that dang necklace as a going-away present, which seemed to warrant a goodbye kiss at her front door, and before he knew what hit him, that innocent kiss exploded into a night of pure firehouse passion.

Not that he would go back and change anything, he wouldn't. He simply needed to stop thinking about it and comparing Helen to other women.

Like, say for instance, Jenny Pickens, who could talk a rutting bull to sleep. Which accounted for why Colt hadn't seen his boys move the trampoline closer to the barn and why when he eventually spotted Joey up on the roof through the kitchen window, after listening to Jenny drone on about her bunion removal ordeal, he near about died right there over Joey's strawberries and cream birthday cake.

"What the—" Colt said as he ran out the back door, past Jenny, who yammered on about the causes of bunions.

Joey's two older brothers, Buddy, who was going on eight years old, and Gavin, who'd recently turned six,

along with several other children on the ground goaded
him to jump down onto the large trampoline they'd managed to move closer to the barn. Colt didn't share their
enthusiasm for the jump and did a record-breaking sprint
toward the barn to try and stop what was sure to be a
horrible miscalculation of a kid's innocent prank.

"Don't you dare!" Colt yelled as he came closer. "Joseph Dodge Granger, you better not jump or there'll be
hell to pay!"

But Joey apparently couldn't hear him and instead
prepared himself for the leap of faith.

He twisted himself around and stood on the edge of
the roof, ignoring his father's plea.

Colt screamed louder this time. "Don't do it, son!"

Other parents, who up until that moment had been
busy partying, took notice of the unfolding events and
were also yelling for Joey not to jump. But if Colt knew
his son, nothing would deter him from going through
with something he started. Joey was even more pigheaded than Colt, and that said a lot.

Just as Joey turned toward his dad with that sly little
smirk he got whenever he was about to do something he
knew he shouldn't, and Colt's heart stopped beating, Travis, Colt's younger brother, suddenly appeared behind
Joey. He reached out, grabbed the boy in midair and the
two of them tumbled down onto the trampoline below.

Colt held his breath as they floated down and landed
in the center of the trampoline, bouncing in a tangle of
limbs, boots and cowboy hats.

No one spoke as Joey and Travis continued to bounce
at least three more times.

Then, in what seemed like an entire lifetime, both
Joey and Travis were upright, reaching for the sky, while

the other kids and party guests cheered and squealed with delight.

"Dumb trampoline," Colt mumbled as he sat down hard on the grass. He moved his black felt hat back on his head, wiped the sweat off his brow with his arm and waited for his heart to stop banging against his rib cage.

Just then, Jenny Pickens sat herself down next to him. "You look as though you could use this." She handed him a bottle of root beer, then proceeded to tell him all about when she'd climbed up an oak tree in a school yard in Boise, her childhood hometown.

First of all, Colt would have preferred a regular beer, and second of all, he was in no mood to listen to her tale. Being too polite to interrupt, he smiled and said, "Thanks. You sure know how to comfort a man."

"That's what everybody says." Then she snorted out her laugh and Colt considered strangling both his brothers.

After a few moments of her yammering, Colt tuned her out and watched as his two other sons joined Joey on the trampoline. Travis had gotten off and was busy supervising the fun.

"Could'a been worse, son," Colt's father, Dodge, said as he knelt on one knee on Colt's other side. Dodge, who towered over most folks at six foot four, sported a thick head of silky white hair, had a walk like John Wayne, a temperament like a slow-moving train and a way of seeing things that generally made a person listen.

Jenny had sprawled herself back on the grass alongside Colt, still talking, apparently not seeing that Dodge had taken root next to Colt. "Wasn't nothing like when you jumped off, thinking you could fly. As I recall, you landed in a heap of horse manure out back. Took a spell to get the scent of horse dung outta your hair."

The memory came rushing back and it wasn't a pleasant one. "Different time. I was older and knew what I was doing. Joey's too young. Could've missed that trampoline completely."

"Your brother made sure he didn't. And thinkin' about it, seems to me you was no bigger than Joey when you jumped. The way I had it figured, landing on that there getup is cleaner. 'Sides, Joey's more like you than you realize. Got a stubborn streak a mile long. I knew it was only a matter of time fore he got up on that there roof. Thought we should be prepared."

Colt stared up at his dad, the noonday sun causing him to squint. Dodge seemed to know what was coming before it came and how to handle it when it arrived. The man always was downright wearisome.

"If you're expecting me to say thank you, I won't. If you hadn't bought that darn thing in the first place, maybe Joey wouldn't have thought to jump."

Dodge chewed on that for a minute. His attention momentarily landed on Jenny, who was busy with the details of a fireman climbing up the oak tree to get to her, branch by branch. Dodge whispered, "She your brothers' doing?"

Colt gave him a little nod.

"They never did have no sense." Then he said, "The way I see it, when dealin' with young bucks, there either *is* or there *ain't. Maybe* won't never do you no good at all."

Colt wanted to argue, needed to argue to blow off the steam that was tearing up his insides, but he spotted Helen Shaw ambling right for him and in an instant, just the sight of her melted away all his anger. Her ruby-colored hair surrounded her beautiful face and covered her shoulders as she made her way closer to him, looking better than ever in her tight black jeans, brown boots and a tan T-shirt featuring a cowgirl on horseback. To say that Colt had it bad for this woman would have been an understatement. To say that he could think of nothing but wicked bedroom thoughts as she approached was more to the point.

Still, now was not the time. It was his son's birthday and said son had pitched himself off the barn roof. The boy needed scolding in the worst way.

Nonetheless, as Helen walked in closer, he knew reprimanding Joey would have to take a backseat for the moment. Dodge was right, as he always was. Joey's descent off the roof had been inevitable. Colt was just happy Dodge had prepared for it.

"Now, there's a mighty fine woman." Dodge patted Colt on the shoulder, and walked away. Colt stood.

Jenny stopped talking and also stood, moving next to Colt.

When Helen finally came within earshot, Colt said, "You left the tour just for Joey's birthday party? We're honored."

He stepped away from Jenny, wanting to take Helen in his arms and never let go, but instead he felt awkward with Jenny once again at his elbow.

Helen stopped a couple feet in front of him. Her deep green eyes sparkled as she gazed over at encroaching Jenny, who had her hand out before Helen could respond to Colt.

"Hi, I'm Jenny Pickens." She rested her other hand on Colt's arm, familiar, as if they were a couple. His instinct was to flick it off like an annoying bug, but he didn't want to be rude. She continued, "I don't think we've ever officially met. You served me drinks a couple times at

Belly Up. Don't you still work there? What tour? Are you in a band? I always wanted to be in a band."

Helen worked at Belly Up Saloon as a waitress and part-time bartender whenever she wasn't on the road. At one point or another she'd probably served half the town a drink of some sort. Everyone seemed to end up at Belly Up for one occasion or another. It was the only real tavern for miles.

She gave Jenny a quick handshake, then let go. No smile. Her reaction to Jenny was as cold as ice on a frozen lake. "Nice to meet you." She turned to Colt with a concerned look on her face. "Can we talk?"

But Jenny answered. "Sure. Why don't we sit down on one of the benches on the front porch. It's nice and shady there."

Colt moved away from Jenny's grip on his arm. "If you'll excuse me, Jenny. This is between Helen and me."

Jenny tilted her head, smiled sweetly and said, "Sure. Don't you worry about me. I'll be fine. Just fine. I'll wait for you on the porch."

She walked away, leaving an awkward silence between Colt and Helen. They both started talking at once. Colt trying to tell her that he just met Jenny today, but his words seemed garbled as he attempted to speak over Helen, who was asking if Jenny was his new girlfriend, a concept that stunned Colt.

Finally they both stopped.

"You first," Colt said.

Helen hesitated for a moment, then said, "That's one brave little boy you have there."

"More like ornery and pigheaded if you ask me."

"Like his father."

"And his father before him. What brings you back to Briggs? Shouldn't you be in Vegas, competing?"

"Actually, Tater's still there. I'm having him transported in a couple days. Something's happened and I'm on my way to Jackson to stay with my parents for a while, but I wanted to stop here first and…"

His stomach pitched as he took a step closer and reached out for her. She stepped back, away from his touch. "Are you okay? What's wrong? Something wrong with your parents?"

She completely befuddled him. His mind raced with scenarios. None of them good.

"Nothing like that." She glanced over at Jenny, now seated on the front porch. "Is there someplace private?"

He chuckled. "Sure, we can try, but at the moment—" he nodded toward Joey and his boys charging straight for them "—that doesn't look too promising."

Joey ran right for him at full speed, calling his name, looking all proud of himself. "Papa! Papa! Did you see me?" He ran smack into Colt as he swooped up his boy in his arms, giving him a tight squeeze, thankful there were no broken bones.

"You had me scared as a jackrabbit with a fox on its trail. Never do that again. You hear me, son? Never."

Joey's face went all serious. His blue eyes instantly lost their sparkle. "But, Papa, it's my fourth birthday and Gramps said you jumped off the roof when you were four. Isn't that what I was supposed to do?"

"Sounds about right to me," Helen said as Colt's other two boys grabbed hold of her with tight hugs. Colt knew how much his boys liked Helen, but he also knew they were a handful when they tackled her like they were doing now.

"Boys, give her some breathing room."

They let go and tackled Colt instead, knocking him to the ground, where they wrestled and tickled him.

"Wait!" Colt yelled over their laughter and squeals. "You boys almost gave me a heart attack. What the heck were you thinking?"

They stopped attacking Colt and Joey got all serious. "Did you have a heart attack, Papa? Should I call nine-one-one?"

"No, I'm fine, but that's beside the point."

"You didn't have a heart attack and I jumped off the roof. That makes me happy. Are you happy?"

Colt sat up and looked Joey in the eyes. "Promise me you'll never, ever do that again."

"Why would I do it again? I could hurt myself."

Helen let out a little laugh. Colt shot her a look. "This is serious." He turned back to his boy. "That's right, son. You could break some bones or worse."

"Of course he could, that's why we moved the trampoline over," Buddy, his oldest, said.

"We're not stupid, Daddy," Gavin chimed in.

"Yeah, Daddy," Helen added.

Colt tried to keep a straight face, but was having a difficult time of it.

"I didn't want to jump into the manure pile like you did," Joey said. "That stinks and I might have missed and landed on the ground. I could crack my head open and die on my birthday. I don't want to die on my birthday. That's no fun. I'd miss out on all the presents and cake. Can we cut my cake now?"

Colt grinned at Joey, unable to stay angry at his youngest for more than five seconds. "Yes. Cake sounds like a good idea." He stood, and his boys stood, as well. "You run and tell your aunt Maggie it's time. She made the cake especially for you."

"It's a real cake, right? She didn't let Aunt Kitty make

it out of broccoli or anything healthy, did she? I won't have to pretend I like it, will I?"

Kitty, Maggie's sister, was an honorary aunt who tended to overdo "green."

"Nope, your aunt Maggie told me it's pure sugar and flour."

"Yay!" Joey yelled and the three boys took off to look for their aunt Maggie, while Colt shook off any lingering tension that had encompassed his body.

"How the heck do parents do it with a whole houseful of kids? Three boys are enough to keep me up all night worrying about what crazy shenanigans they might come up with next. I never even considered a planned jump off the barn roof. If I had any more kids, I'd probably go insane."

He felt thankful he'd had the wherewithal to take care of that possibility years ago.

Besides, when his beautiful wife died in childbirth with Joey, he'd decided then and there he never, ever wanted to be responsible for another pregnancy as long as he lived.

He turned to Helen. "Now, what did you want to talk to me about?"

Chapter Two

It had taken Helen three days to drive to Briggs, Idaho, from Vegas, and on the way she'd taken four home pregnancy tests, gone through three boxes of tissue and arrived on the Granger ranch puffy-eyed, solidly pregnant and homeless. She had leased out her little house for six months to a family of four, who had happily settled in.

The drive had been grueling due to all the stops she'd made not only to pee a million times, but because she could barely see the road through her tears. She had cried almost the entire drive back, not so much over the pregnancy itself but more about the stifling fear she felt over being someone's mom. Heck, even though she had recently turned twenty-eight years old, she could barely take care of herself, let alone a whole other person.

Helen decided that telling Colt he had fathered baby number four after he about had a coronary when his youngest jumped off the barn roof might have been the wrong moment to break the news. Then there was always his date, a woman totally wrong for Colt, who seemed a tad bit overly protective, and clingy.

Not exactly the optimum time to tell a cowboy who had taken the radical step to ensure he would never father another child that he had indeed impregnated another woman.

So instead, Helen made her excuses and abruptly left the party right after Jenny Pickens sashayed back to Colt and draped her scrawny little arm around his shoulder.

That was more than four months ago.

Since that day, Helen had secured Tater at M & M Riding School in Briggs, where she had boarded him for the past couple of years when she wasn't on the road, then driven to her parents' house in Jackson, Wyoming, less than an hour away. She'd spent the majority of her time allowing her friends and family to shamelessly dote on her every whim while she adjusted to her new life.

Apparently she'd needed all that doting, because only in the past few weeks had she finally reached the total-acceptance stage. She was good with her pregnancy now, had gone through the five stages of mourning over her old, carefully planned life and was looking forward to all that motherhood had to offer...at least on her good days.

Her sweet and affectionate stepmom, Janet, had provided her with an e-reader and loaded it up with every conceivable book related to pregnancy and the baby's first year. Some of it soothed Helen's concerns, while others she'd read, especially details of the delivery, gave her night sweats. She dreaded getting a tooth filled; how on earth was she ever going to push out an entire baby?

The concept crippled her. So instead, she put the e-reader in a drawer and told herself she'd deal with it later.

Her logical electronic engineer dad had helped get her finances in order, and had generously contributed to her dwindling bank account so she no longer had to worry about funds. Her cousins, aunts, uncles and benevolent friends had all rallied around her with support and nonstop love. Helen felt truly blessed.

Now all she had to do was tell Colt Granger he was the father, a fact that everyone in her circle kept nudging her to do, but she kept resisting. Each time she had screwed up enough courage to tell him, she found a hundred reasons why she couldn't make the phone call or drive that long hour to Briggs. Add to that an element that he might not believe her, and it was everything Helen could do to even think about how she would broach the subject.

What finally forced her to have to cowgirl up and face him was an official phone call from Mrs. Milton, one of the owners from the riding school. After thirty years in business, the school, land and private home was up for sale. The owners had decided to retire, a fact that saddened Helen more than she thought possible. The M & M Riding School had been her summer home for most of her teen years and the arena at the school had served as her main training ground ever since she'd taken cowboy mounted shooting seriously.

She was informed that Tater was one of only three horses still left that needed to be moved. "We kept him as long as we could, honey, hoping that we'd get a quick sale and you could board him with the new owners. Unfortunately, that isn't the case, so you'll have to move him in the next few days. Sorry to put you under such pressure, but our new house in town is ready and we want to get settled in before the holidays."

"Not a problem," Helen told her, thinking she'd move him over to her cousin Milo's place in Briggs until she could find him a more permanent home. She knew he wouldn't mind. He'd boarded Tater before and loved him almost as much as Helen did.

The call required immediate action, and so did her growing condition.

It was time she took charge, moved her horse and told Colt the truth despite her apprehensions.

"I'll be there tomorrow," she told Mrs. Milton. She disconnected, walked out onto her parents' back porch, gazed out at the bright blue sky, the surrounding mountains and contemplated Colt Granger.

She hadn't seen or heard anything about Colt since Joey's birthday. He'd called a couple times, but she hadn't returned his calls. She'd been thrown into a life-long responsibility with a man who was dating other women, Jenny Pickens just to name one. Now that he'd started dating again, who knew how many more women were chomping at the bit to be in his little black book. For all she knew, practically every single woman in the entire county had made the cut. It was only a matter of time until he found Ms. Right, and it certainly wouldn't be her.

Helen was more in the Ms. All Wrong category, and for now, that suited her just fine. They'd made love exactly once. Okay, so it was powerful and more passionate than what she'd ever experienced with any other man, but that didn't mean they could ever have a viable relationship. For starters, he had three sons, three ornery, unmanageable sons. She had fears and apprehensions about one child, let alone three more.

Her baby moved and kicked as she sat back rubbing her tummy, grateful that she could trust her family with her secret until she was ready to tell Colt. She decided to spend a few days with her cousin Milo Gump in Briggs.

Everyone in the family had an open invitation to stay on Milo's ranch. He liked the company, especially now that his parents had retired to a smaller place in Oregon, and his sister had moved to Austin, Texas, with her new husband.

Her thirty-year-old cousin was a man who was generous to a fault, and the one person in the entire world she could trust with a secret.

"YOU TOLD MAGGIE GRANGER, Colt's sister-in-law, that I'm pregnant?" Helen couldn't believe Milo could betray her after she'd told him several times not to tell anyone until she personally broke the news to Colt.

"You can't exactly hide it," Milo said, staring at her prominent belly. She wore a stretchy green top that caressed her baby bump, boot-cut maternity jeans and her favorite tan-colored cowgirl boots.

"That's not the point. I drove straight here. No one in this gossip-centered town has seen me yet."

"Jackson is only a hop-skip away. It ain't exactly out of drivin' range. Anyone from Briggs could've seen you."

"If someone had seen me, I would know about it."

"Calm down," Milo said, a look of guilt on his chubby face. "I merely told her you'd been taking it easy for a while, staying with your parents in Jackson until the baby came. I didn't say a word about Colt being its daddy."

Helen stared up at Milo from the brown leather sofa in his Western-style living room. She had finally gotten somewhat comfortable after having spent the past hour getting her stomach to settle down long enough so she could eat a bowl of vegetable soup he'd prepared for her that was now getting cold on his coffee table.

She'd driven in the previous night, and ever since she'd arrived her already sensitive stomach seemed to be in a continual state of agitation.

Sort of like her nerves.

"How could you think this information wouldn't get back to Colt?"

Milo plopped down in his recliner across from her, the chair groaning under his weight. He was one of those big guys, not really fat, just big-boned, with a six-foot-five height that would intimidate almost anyone who came his way. He had a sweet face that told anyone who came near him that he was a teddy bear, until you got him riled. Then he was a force to be reckoned with.

Still, Milo was a gentle giant, and Helen loved him to pieces…until this very moment.

"She's the one who asked me why you wasn't at the fair. You know it's Spud Week and everybody's down to the fairgrounds for the fair. It's obvious that you've been missing. 'Specially since you didn't participate in the Spud Tug this year. Our team won, by the way."

The Spud Tug was a tug-of-war over a pit of mashed potatoes instead of mud. Helen usually participated on Milo's team.

"Your team always wins."

"I know," he chided and Helen gazed over at his latest Spudphy, a six inch high golden-colored russet potato man wearing a cowboy hat, cowboy boots on his tiny legs and a belt around his wide midsection. There were at least ten Spudphys perched on Milo's bookshelf, along with many other potato-oriented awards.

Next to Christmas, Spud Week in Briggs was the biggest celebration going. Schools closed, businesses shut down early and everyone headed out to the fairgrounds in honor of the almighty potato.

"You could have told her that I took a fall and injured myself. That I'm suddenly allergic to potatoes. I don't know. Anything would've been better than telling her the truth. Did she say anything after you told her?"

"All she said was, *I understand.* And then she walked off to meet up with her sister, Kitty."

"She said, *I understand.*"

"Yeah, that's good, right?" His face lit up, and he looked like a little boy eager to please with his curly dark hair falling over his ears, and down his collar.

Helen stood, anxious to get to the fair to find Colt. She knew he'd be there all day with his boys. There were always a lot of games for kids to participate in and she knew from previous years that his boys liked to join in as many as they could.

"No, that's very bad. I've got to get to Colt before rumors start to fly."

"Well, I told you to tell him when you visited months ago." He slid into a reclining position and turned on his favorite TV show on the food channel, its glamorous host, who he would run away with in a heartbeat, popped up on the screen. Today she would be cooking up a backyard picnic and Milo had every intention of sitting and watching the entire show with his notepad and pen at the ready.

"I know, but the timing wasn't right. Joey had just nearly killed himself."

The opening shots of the chef's Texas ranch came up on the sixty-inch flat-screen TV. Milo increased the volume. He loved her Italian theme song.

"She's chopping pineapples and cabbage today for coleslaw, and I love to watch her chop things. Best part of the show."

"That's a little sick."

"No, it ain't. Not the way you think anyway. I'm a horrible chopper. She's a master."

The theme song ended and the host stood in her kitchen, picked up her chopping knife and began chopping away.

"Look at the way she handles that cabbage, and that big knife. She's got a real talent for chopping. It's an art."

Helen stared at Milo in disbelief.

"Since when do you care about slicing vegetables?"

"Since I entered the show's contest. If I win, I get to fly to Texas to her ranch for a full two days of cooking lessons, then dinner with her out on her private veranda. That would be heaven."

"You only eat hot dogs, burgers, spuds and an occasional steak."

"Yeah, but a man can dream, can't he?" He closed his eyes as the show went to a commercial. After a second or two, a wide smile creased his lips. "Besides, I'm learning how to cook because of her."

She stuck a hand to her hip. "Be careful what you wish for, big cousin."

"As careful as you are, little cousin." He opened his eyes and turned to her. "Now get yourself over to that there fair and tell your man you're carryin' his child. Then let him do the right thing and everybody'll be happy."

"That's not why I'm telling him."

"Oh?" His eyebrow went up.

"He has a right to know, is all."

"Sweetheart, you've had a crush on Colt Granger since you was kids."

"Yes, and it's still a crush."

He turned, looked down at her belly and grinned. "Seriously?"

"It was just one crazy night. Nothing more."

"Looks like a lot more to me."

Helen sighed, turned on her heels, grabbed her purse off the coffee table and headed for the door. Sometimes her cousin could be so dang frustrating.

IT WAS A PERFECT Teton Valley fall day, a clear blue sky, a cool breeze skipping down from the surrounding mountains and the tall grasses elegantly bending with each breeze. The air smelled sweet, and the sun tried its best to warm Colt, but there was a deep freeze that clung to his heart. His sister-in-law, Maggie, had mentioned that Helen was pregnant. If it was true, he figured the father had to be some no-account cowpoke from the circuit, or why else would she be living with her folks?

But Colt knew Helen fairly well so he absolutely refused to believe it, and wouldn't believe it until he heard it from Helen herself. Colt knew enough about town rumors to know they were only half-truths, but with this bit of gossip he was hopeful the entire tale was a fabrication. And until he heard otherwise, he intended to try to enjoy the piglet races with his boys, who were somewhat behaved on this fine evening.

Colt and Buddy, his oldest, who had to tell everyone he would soon be eight and a half, sat side by side in the third row on the metal bleachers. Colt's other two sons, Joey and six-year-old Gavin, sat on the other side of Buddy. Normally, Colt would sit in the middle with his boys flanking his sides, but ever since the roof incident, and Colt's stern warning before he tucked them into bed each night, his boys seemed to be more agreeable than pups in a basket.

The piglet races were one of the highlights of the fair, and the crowded stands were testament to that fact. Black-and-white silks adorned the small oval track. Wood shavings encircled the floor of the track that couldn't be more than a hundred and fifty feet around. With five rows of metal bleachers on three sides, it would soon be standing room only.

Four baby oinkers adorned in various colors of brown, green, pink and black, with their big ears flapping, were hand-carried out onto the track from a colorful thirty-foot trailer, introduced to the excited audience, then placed in separate cages that sat on the starting line. Colt, his boys and the audience cheered, clapped and whistled as the Swinemaster, a rugged-looking cowboy sporting a handlebar mustache and a large white classic cowboy hat, announced the upcoming race.

"Racing as piglet number one we have Bob Beboar. Number two is our darling Josephine Hoglarson, number three is Stephanie Porkman and finally number four is the lovely Olive Oinkly."

The crowd reacted with hoots and whistles just as Colt spotted Helen heading right for him. She looked about as pretty as the first spring rose. She wore her favorite straw cowboy hat and if he wasn't mistaken, he could make out the necklace he'd given her around her pretty neck.

His heart raced.

His palms were clammy.

Suddenly all he could think of was her naked body

lying under him as he kissed her. The scent of her. The feel of her silky skin. Her warm touch on his—

The crowd parted and he spotted her prominent baby bump.

His breath hitched.

"Hey, good-lookin'," Lana Thomson said as she made her way toward Colt. He'd forgotten that Travis had set him up with Lana for the festival. It suddenly dawned on him that he was supposed to have met her near the front entrance to the wine booths a good twenty minutes ago, but with everything else going on around him at the fair, he'd completely forgotten.

"Lana, hi!" he said, jumping up to greet her as he desperately tried to think up an excuse for why meeting her had completely slipped his mind. He wished his brothers would stop trying to pair him with every available girl in town. Of all people, Lana Thomson, who was about as right for him as a Vegas showgirl.

"Good thing I ran into your dad or I would've thought you stood me up. I know I was a little late getting here, but that couldn't be helped. A girl has to look her best on her first date with a Granger. The competition is steep, sweetie, but from what I hear, the rewards are just this side of heaven." She gave him a slow once-over, lingering a little too long on body parts she shouldn't be staring at in a public place, especially with his boys sitting next to him.

Once again, because of his brothers' incessant meddling, he found himself in a troublesome situation.

"I need four volunteers from the stands," the Swinemaster bellowed. "One from each section!"

"Colt Granger, we need to talk," Helen said as she

approached. She spoke with such force Colt near about hopped forward as if he were on a spring.

"Sure," Colt answered as he tried to move around Lana. "Will you excuse me?"

He couldn't really get to Helen because of all the kids who were now standing around him, cheering and laughing in anticipation of the race.

"You, sir, come on down to the front," he heard the Swinemaster say.

Colt's son Buddy nudged him, giggling. "He wants you, Dad."

All three of his boys were hysterical with laughter.

"He wants you to come down and pick a piggy for the race," Gavin told him.

"Pick number one, Papa, Bob Beboar. He's the biggest," Joey ordered, then burst out laughing again.

But Colt couldn't seem to move. Way too many things were going on at the same time.

"Daddy, hurry up. You're holding up the race," Gavin ordered.

"What? No. This is a kid's race," Colt mumbled, feeling like a first-class fool.

"Come on down, sir. Come get your snout on," the Swinemaster shouted, holding up a rubber pig snout attached to a white stretchy band. Then the Swinemaster proceeded to pick three other volunteers, kids well under the age of ten.

Feeling completely discomfited, Colt made his way down the metal stairs with everyone cheering him on as they made a path for him to get by.

When he passed Helen, he said, "I didn't think it was true."

"That's why we need to talk," she said over the hoots

coming from the crowd. "If you can tear yourself away from Lana Thomson long enough for a private conversation."

"What? No. You have the wrong idea. We're not—"

"It seems one of our team captains is holding up the race," the Swinemaster bellowed. "Sir, we need you to pick out your favorite piggy."

Everyone in Colt's section began hooting and yelling for him to get down to the front.

"Don't leave," he told Helen, hoping she wouldn't lose interest in talking to him because of Lana.

"I'll be here," she said, but she didn't look happy.

He walked off toward the Swinemaster and the piglet cages at the start line. It seemed as if everyone in the entire arena was cheering for him. Of all the confounded situations for him to find himself in, this certainly was not one he had anticipated when he left the ranch that morning.

The Swinemaster handed Colt and the three children, two boys and a girl, their rubber snouts. Colt stared at it for a moment, as if there was no way he was slipping the silly thing on his face, until the other kids started poking him to put it on. He really had little choice in the matter. He slipped off his cowboy hat, and snapped the contraption around his head, making sure his snout was securely in place over his nose.

"Of all the crazy things…"

The audience seemed to love the entire spectacle and continued to cheer and laugh. Whatever friends he had in the audience called out his name, then whistled. He wondered if he would ever be able to live it down.

"And what's your name, sonny?" the Swinemaster

asked Colt, thrusting the microphone in front of his face, obviously milking the situation.

"Colt."

"And how old are you, Colt?"

"You're kidding, right?"

"Nope. How old are you?"

"Too old."

"Apparently you're not too old to wear a snout."

Colt could feel himself blush as he adjusted his snout. "Apparently."

The crowd roared with laughter as Colt decided to roll with it.

"And seeing as how you're the tallest, we'll give you first pick."

"My boys told me to pick Bob Beboar."

His section clapped and cheered as the Swinemaster's male helper secured a large number one on either side of the baby swine.

Then the other kids were asked the same questions while Colt watched as Helen was offered a seat in the first row. Soon his three boys had made their way down to where Helen sat and squeezed in around her, with Joey sitting on her lap. His boys seemed to enjoy being around Helen, and he felt the feeling was mutual on her part. She could always get them to laugh and they loved hearing her stories from being on the circuit. If it wasn't for her gypsy soul, he probably would've considered seriously dating her a long time ago.

Lana now sat alone up in the stands, straining to get his attention. He caught her waving out of the corner of his eye. When he finally glanced her way, she threw him a kiss, keeping her cherry-colored lips puckered while she pretended to blow the kiss his way. Colt didn't ex-

actly know what to do with that, so he grinned and nodded, not wanting to seem rude. She instantly feigned a
demure pose and blinked her eyes several times.

To Colt's complete dismay he realized she thought
he was flirting with her. And to compound matters, it
was at that exact moment when Helen glanced back at
Lana, then back at Colt. He caught the snide look on her
face just before she said something to his boys, stood
and scooted Joey into her seat, then headed for the exit.

Colt didn't want her to go, not without talking to her
about her baby. Plus, he really didn't want her to think
there was anything between him and Lana but air.

"No! Helen, wait!" he shouted, and that was all it took
for his boys to go tearing after her at the exact moment
the piglets took off on the track.

What happened next was something the townsfolk
would talk about for years to come.

In Joey's enthusiasm to catch up with Helen, he
jumped the barrier to try to stop her. His foot must have
gotten tangled up on the piglet-size metal fence, and just
as Bob Beboar, who happened to be in the lead, along
with Stephanie Porkman on his tail, rounded the turn,
the barrier flopped down and all four piglets ran off in
different directions into the stunned crowd.

Soon piglet mayhem erupted while Colt tried to catch
his boys. The entire throng of people went completely
hog wild, with adults, kids, pigs and the Swinemaster
trying their darnedest to catch the little critters before
they disrupted the entire festival.

Within minutes, Colt managed to grab a hold of Bob
Beboar in one arm and catch Joey around the waist in
his other arm. He couldn't tell which squirmed more,
the piggy or his son, both equally angry for the sudden

loss of freedom. Gavin and Buddy were too slippery for him, and disappeared chasing down the piglets with Helen in hot pursuit.

"I'll catch the boys," she yelled back at Colt.

Lana, on the other hand, managed to remain unruffled, that is until Colt walked up to her as she stood chatting with one of the pig wranglers who'd stayed behind, undoubtedly, to collect the returned piglets and to protect the other sixteen swine from escaping in the confusion.

"Thanks," the wrangler said, tipping his black hat in Colt's direction then grabbing hold of the wiggling piglet with both hands.

Soon Olive Oinkly was returned, along with Josephine Hoglarson, and the pandemonium seemed to be dying down in their immediate area. But Colt could hear screams and roars coming from the booths where the crafts and various vintners displayed their finest.

With judicious hesitation, Colt put Joey down, but held on to the back of his cotton tee.

"Let me go, Papa. I want to help catch the last piggy."

"You'll stay right here with me, son. You've done more than your share of hell-raising for one day. Besides, don't you think you owe this man an apology for letting his pigs get away?"

Joey looked up at Colt, sincerity shining on his cherub face. "I didn't mean to let them get away, Papa. Honest, I didn't. My foot got caught."

The wrangler, a big guy in his early twenties, his blond curly hair popping out in various angles from under his hat, stooped down to Joey's level. "You're more of a handful than these baby pigs. Don't you know better than to jump on the track when the piglets are running? They could get hurt."

"Yes, sir," Joey said, not looking at the wrangler, who had already carefully placed Bob Beboar back in his cage.

Colt gave Joey a little nudge.

"I'm sorry. I wouldn't hurt those little piggies for anything." Big tears streamed down Joey's cheeks. He wiped them away with the backs of his hands. It near about broke Colt's heart, but he knew his son had to learn these lessons the hard way.

"Tell you what," the wrangler said. "I so appreciate you telling me that you're sorry that you can help me make sure all the cages are locked tight. That is, if your dad says it's okay."

Joey looked up at Colt, the last of his tears still glistening on his rosy cheeks. "Go on, son, but you mind him."

"I will, Papa. I promise."

They didn't go far, only a few feet in front of Colt, when Lana stepped into his view.

"Colt, honey, as much as I'd like to get to know you better—" she stepped in closer "—and I'd really like to get to know you—" she slid her hands up his chest and leaned in even closer "—it couldn't possibly work between us, sweetheart. I don't do children well, and I especially couldn't do *your* children. Unless, of course, you agree to send them off to school somewhere. I'd be good with that, especially if you wore that nose to bed. It could be kind of kinky."

She moaned sensually, and Colt coughed loudly. He gently removed her hands from his chest. "As much as your offer intrigues me, I'm a package deal."

"Shame, we could've had so much fun!"

She stepped away as Helen walked up with Buddy and Gavin in tow. Buddy carried a complaining, wiggly Stephanie Porkman, as Lana's eyes lit up on Helen's round stomach.

As IF HELEN hadn't juggled enough of her emotions deal-ing with Jenny Pickens, now she had to accept Lana Thomson, of all people. Not only was Lana the biggest flirt in the county, and possibly the entire state, it was a well-known fact that Lana had a zero tolerance for chil-dren. But there she was stroking Colt's chest while she laid it on as thick as molasses.

The boys went off with the wrangler, leaving Helen alone with Colt and Lana. Not a good situation. Helen wanted out of there.

Now.

"So the rumors were true," Lana told her as she took a step away from Colt. "That's why you didn't stay on the circuit. Shame. From what I hear you were close this time. But I understand." She tried her best to feign a mask of compassion, but Helen knew it was all a show for Colt's sake. "Heaven knows it's a tough and lonely road. It takes stamina and grit to be a champion like me. Two attributes not many women share."

She stuck her thumb behind her gold championship buckle, in case Helen missed the large trophy holding up her designer jeans. Lana had won it for women's barrel racing a few years ago, and ever since then she took great joy in rubbing Helen's nose in it every time they met.

She and Helen had both started out as barrel racers when they were kids. They even attended the M & M Riding School together, but once Helen saw her first female mounted shooter she was smitten and left bar-rel racing to pursue her real passion, cowboy mounted shooting. Lana had tried to convince her to stay, telling her cowboy mounted shooting was too tough to ever master, but once Helen made up her mind on something, there was no turning back. Even the Miltons, the couple who owned the riding school, had tried to convince her not to do it, but as time went on, they both came around and gave her the training she needed to succeed.

Problem was, now that she was having a baby, that cowboy mounted shooting trophy buckle seemed next to impossible to ever win, which played right into Lana's nasty little one-upmanship.

"The only thing *you* share with other women is their men. Now if you two will excuse me, I've got to get back to my cousin's ranch."

Helen made a move to leave but Colt stopped her. "Wait. Please don't go. Lana was just leaving. Weren't you, Lana?"

Lana shrugged. "I guess so, but Colt, honey, if you ever change your mind, my offer still stands."

And she sashayed off to talk to the Swinemaster, who had since returned.

"Can we try this again?" Colt said to Helen.

Helen knew better than to tell him she was carrying baby number four in a public place. "I don't think this is the right time."

"How about we meet for dinner sometime? Just you and me? Someplace quiet and refined. I'll get Dodge to watch my boys."

He looked so sexy Helen wanted to melt into his arms, until Gavin came running up to him. "Daddy! Daddy! You gotta come quick. Joey climbed into one of the cages with a piggy and got stuck. They're gonna call the fire department to come get him out, but I said you could do it. Daddy, you have to hurry. He's crying."

"Of all the…" Colt turned to Helen. "I'm sorry. Friday night at seven?"

"Sure," she said.

"Daddy, come on. Joey's real scared." Gavin yanked on his father's hand.

"You better go," Helen told him.

"I'll pick you up at Milo's."

"But how did you know…"

Unfortunately, before she could ask him her silly question, he was sprinting toward the piglet cages with Gavin leading the way.

Of course Colt knew she was staying with Milo, just like he probably had already known she was pregnant. The one question still to be answered could only be: Who was the father?

She could imagine the rampant speculation on that one.

The good thing in all of this was she and Colt now had an actual date, a date without his boys, set in a more sedate environment. Somewhere where she would have plenty of opportunity to slowly spill the truth in such a way that Colt could accept it, perhaps maybe even embrace it.

The reality of the undeniable facts hit her hard as she looked on to see a fire engine arrive to free Joey from the piglet cage. Undoubtedly, her baby was another boy, even though she held on to the unlikely notion that it might be a girl. She hadn't wanted to officially know the sex of her baby when the doctor had offered to tell her during an ultrasound. Instead, reason told her it was a boy. That Colt only made boys, but wishful thinking conjured up a sweet baby girl.

Now watching Colt and his boys caught up in another

tangle of male orneriness only increased her longing for a temperate little girl.

She saw Colt offer to help the two firemen release Joey. One of the firemen spoke to Colt and he took a few steps back while keeping his other two sons away from the piglet cage. A small crowd had gathered to watch as Colt shifted his weight from one foot to the other waiting for Joey to be cut free. Red lights twirled, kids whistled, swine oinked as Buddy and Gavin strained to get at their brother.

She took a deep breath and slowly let it out, trying to regain some shred of composure, trying to hold back her growing fear, but most of all trying once again to come to terms with the reality: she was going to be mother to Colt's child.

The crowd cheered as Joey was released from the cage. Colt picked up his boy, who hugged his dad. Then Colt, pig snout still dangling around his neck, and his sons walked off in the opposite direction.

It was in that instant she wondered if telling Colt about his fourth baby was actually necessary.

Chapter Three

Colt pulled his red ranch truck alongside the for sale sign two miles off Highway 33, turned off the ignition and stepped out onto the packed dirt road that led onto the property. He and his brother Travis were scoping out yet another spread for the potato storage facility his family and two other local growers were planning on building before next year's crops came in. This was the third property he'd seen so far and he still had one more to go. It had been a huge decision for the Grangers and for the two other farmers, but a necessary one. The facility they now used was outdated, and last year each family had lost a substantial part of their crops due to mold and rot from temperature fluctuation inside the facility. They expected the same would happen this year, and each family was prepared to take the hit, but they couldn't sustain the loss much after that. They had to break ground on the new building by early spring or it wouldn't be ready in time for next year's crops.

On top of raising his high-spirited boys, running the Granger ranch and managing the yearly potato crop, Colt had also taken up the challenge of finding the appropriate piece of land for the new facility.

"This looks good," Travis declared as he slammed the passenger door shut and walked over to Colt. Travis was the wild one in the family who cared more about partying with his many girlfriends rather than working the ranch. Getting him to join Colt on these property excursions was about as easy as pinning down smoke and Colt didn't want to do or say anything that might make him drift away.

Colt needed to really look at the property close-up. He'd already scoped it out from the air in his Cessna Skyhawk and now he was looking to make sure he still liked what he saw. He had to be sure there was a good road in, easy access from the highway and several acres of flat land for the buildings.

"We can't jump to that conclusion just yet, little brother. There are a lot of factors to consider." This was Colt's first real chance to take over the business from his dad, and he didn't want to mess it up. Dodge had given over all his other duties to Colt, but the business end of the ranch still rested on Dodge's shoulders. Colt knew it was only a matter of time before Dodge would relinquish that duty as well, and he wanted to be prepared for it.

Travis had taken over the care of the livestock and the upkeep of the buildings. He was a crackerjack carpenter who could build or rebuild almost anything. Blake would help out with the yearly potato crop, and sometimes help with wrangling up the livestock, but for the most part, the day-to-day challenge of the massive ranch and farm had fallen on Colt's shoulders.

Not that he minded. It was the life he'd chosen. He merely needed his brothers and Dodge to trust him with his decisions, and to have his back whenever he needed them to.

Plus, he needed a good woman by his side, a woman like Helen, when she wasn't trying to chase after that darn championship. Now that she was going to have a baby with some other dude, he had to rethink his feelings for her. He didn't know why she agreed to dinner with him or why she wanted to talk to him, but he was sure as heck going to find out.

Helen was the kind of woman who did things on her own terms in her own time, so this baby was sure causing him a mountain of wonder.

"You've been struggling over this decision for two months now," Travis countered. "Time is coming up short if we're going to have this thing up and running for next year's crops."

They walked side by side across the open land. It was good and flat for a nice long stretch before it banked upward. The ground was covered in short wild grass, some rocks and stones. Nothing that couldn't be cleared for a sizable building.

But Colt still wasn't sure.

"It's got to be right. I won't spend everybody's hard-earned money on something less than perfect. This new place has to last us a lot of years."

They strolled along on the wild grass, Colt thinking he needed to wait and see what the surveyor he'd hired had to say about it.

Travis shook his head. "You think too much. Always have. It's like you need to walk a mile to find a place to spit."

"I'm cautious, is all."

"You can't see through a ladder." Travis picked up a stone and flung it over the land, as if he was skipping it over water. The stone bounced a couple times before it landed. Colt never could do that, even on water.

"I'm getting the feeling you're not talking about this piece of land."

"Glad you caught up."

Colt turned to his brother. "What are you trying to say?"

"I'm trying to tell you that Blake and me have been trying to find you a woman now for going on near six months. There's been some mighty fine ladies willing to take on you and your rowdy boys, but none of them seem to pass the first date."

"Lana Thomson wanted to send my boys to a boarding school."

"Might do 'em some good."

Colt picked up his speed. "Not sending my sons away. Our dad stuck by us when our mom passed, and I'm doing the same."

Travis skipped another stone. This time it only served to aggravate Colt, making him wonder why he'd brought Travis on this land run in the first place.

"What about Helen? She'd be good with them boys of yours."

"She's out of the picture."

"She won't be once she wins that buckle. I imagine it'll settle her right down."

Colt was thinking Travis hadn't heard the news about Helen's condition. "There's something else that's going on with Helen."

"I know all about her being in a family way. What I heard, she's planning on raising that baby on her own. The baby's daddy don't want no part of it. Might be a good time for you to step in and make your case."

"Where'd you hear that?"

"Lana Thompson."

Colt laughed. "I'm surprised you'd even listen to her kind of talk."

"I'm not saying I do and I'm not saying I don't, but there's gotta be something to it or why else would Helen be living with her folks over in Jackson instead of married to her man?"

"Only Helen can answer that."

"Have you asked her?"

"I was busy shoring up my boys after the fair. Timing wasn't right."

"It all goes back to what I said. You think too much."

"We have a date for Friday night. I'm taking her to Champaign Taste. We'll talk then."

Travis slung his arm around his brother's shoulder. "What's your plan?"

"Plan? Dinner's my plan. She tells me what she wants to say then I drive her back to Milo's. Anything more than that isn't any of your business."

"Maybe so, but if you're feeling a little rusty, I can give you some pointers."

"Getting pointers from you would be like getting pointers from a pup at his mama's tit."

Travis laughed. "Good one, big brother."

"I thought so."

"Is that what you're wearing?" Milo asked as Helen descended the stairs. She wore dark blue jeans, her tan Justin boots and a sky-blue Western maternity shirt. Her hair curled out of a black cowgirl hat.

"It's just dinner in town with Colt. Nothing fancy, I'm sure."

She'd stressed over what to wear ever since Colt had asked her on this impromptu date. She'd tried on everything in her suitcase. She'd even considered a long dress, but then thought it too fancy. Nothing seemed right so she stuck with her tried-and-true jeans and a shirt. She felt comfortable in jeans and a shirt, and tonight of all nights she wanted to be comfortable.

Milo stood next to his recliner, ready to attack it with his full-size body. It was his night off from Spud Drive-In, located on the outskirts of town, where he worked the concession stand a few nights a week during the summer. It got him out of the house and forced him to talk to his neighbors, which he sometimes didn't like doing. Milo had no interest in a nine-to-five job due to an inheritance from his grandfather on his dad's side, which made him "comfortable," as he liked to say. On his free nights, he usually spent them catching up on his recorded shows.

"Did he say it wouldn't be fancy?"

"No, but why should it be?"

"A man don't ask you to dinner then take you for fast food. It usually means a tablecloth and a server. I'm just sayin'." He shrugged.

"Fine! I'll rethink my outfit."

"Have you thought about what you're gonna say?"

"Of course I have."

She really hadn't, but she didn't want to get into it with Milo. He was a man of preparedness and believed you should always practice before you attempted anything that might be awkward, and that naturally included telling Colt about his baby.

"Try it out on me. I'm a good judge of these things."

Helen crossed her arms over her chest and let out a frustrated sigh. "Colt, I'm pregnant with your baby."

"And…"

"And nothing. That's all I have."

"It stinks."

"It's the truth."

"Yeah, but you can ease him into it with small talk first."

"For instance?" She shifted her weight to one hip and tapped her foot a few times.

"I don't know… Tell him he looks good in his new hat."

"What new hat?"

"The one he bought yesterday at Mad Hatter's."

"How do you know this?"

"It's a small town."

"Damn, it's smaller than I thought. This is crazy. A guy can't even buy a new hat without everybody knowing about it."

"And a single girl can't waltz back into town with a baby belly and not expect everyone to speculate on the circumstances."

She sighed, unfolded her arms and plopped down onto the sofa, feeling as if the entire town knew every detail of her life and she hadn't even told anyone a thing about it. "I give. Just tell me what I should say and I'll do my best to make it sound as if I came up with it on my own."

"Before I help you out, maybe you should girl up first. What time is your date?"

"'Girl up'? Have you been hanging around with Amanda Fittswater again? You know that girl will be the death of you. She's still wet behind the ears."

"She's just a friend."

"She's not even twenty-one yet."

"Turned twenty-two three weeks ago, and we're not talking about me. We're talking about you and Colt."

She crossed her arms again. "There is no 'me and Colt.' There's only his baby that needs to be discussed."

"You make it sound as if you're somehow not attached to that there young'un."

"Believe me, I'm attached, just not to Colt."

"You look mighty attached to Colt Granger from where I'm standing."

"Well, stand someplace else 'cause we aren't a couple, never have been a couple and probably never will be a couple."

"You used the word *probably*."

"Yeah? So?"

"That means—"

The doorbell rang and the sound startled Helen. "He's fifteen minutes early."

Milo peeked out of the side window. "It's not Colt. You still have time to change."

Helen headed for the door, but Milo beat her to it, whisking past her faster than she'd ever seen his cumbersome body move. She stood to the side of the door, not able to see who stood on the other side when Milo opened it. Immediately his face lit up as if he were a kid staring at a Christmas tree. Amanda Fittswater's distinctive voice echoed through the living room. "Hey, cuddles. Are you ready?"

"Cuddles?" Helen whispered when Milo glanced her way.

He blushed.

"Hey, Amanda. Yeah, I'm ready. Let's go."

Helen came around to the front of the door. "Aren't you going to invite her in?"

"Hey, Helen," Amanda said when their eyes met. She still looked like a kid with a fresh scrubbed face, a lean body, mahogany hair streaked with pink highlights cut extra short, bright pink lipstick, red minishorts, a black long-sleeved sweater and tan cowboy boots. "Like, I can't. The movie starts in less than ten minutes. But we'll catch up next time. Come on over to Holy Rollers and I'll give you a free muffin."

She'd worked at Holy Rollers, the local doughnut and pastry shop, ever since it opened. Her aunt owned the place and everyone knew she was grooming Amanda to one day take it over when she retired, that is if she could keep Amanda interested.

She grabbed Milo's hand and the two of them walked out the door and down the street in the direction of Galaxy Theater, while Helen stood there and watched. Amanda jumped and skipped around him like a puppy vying for attention.

Oh, yeah, they were just friends all right.

That's when she spotted Colt's white SUV turning onto the street. She left the front door wide open for him, and raced up the stairs to change clothes and practice how she would tell him about their baby.

"Hi, Colt, I love your new hat. Colt, is that a new hat? Wow, that new hat looks great on you. By the way, did I happen to mention you're the daddy to the baby I'm carrying?" She stomped up the last three stairs knowing that telling Colt about their baby was the single most difficult thing she'd ever had to do.

COLT PULLED HIS SUV over to the curb a block away from Milo's place in order to give his boys one more talk before he picked up Helen for their date. He hadn't planned on bringing his boys, but Dodge had a "previous engagement" that he neglected to tell Colt about until a couple hours ago. Mrs. Abernathy, the older, semi-retired nurse who Colt could always depend on as his backup babysitter, was also busy that night, and both his brothers along with Maggie and Scout had tickets to a truck and tractor pull over in Idaho Falls, so he was stuck having to bring his boys.

If he'd had more time to tell Helen about the change in

circumstances, he would have called her and broken the date. Unfortunately, he'd assumed his dad, who rarely went anywhere but the barn in the evening, would be available to look after his boys. He never would have guessed in a million years the old man wouldn't be available. No way would he call Helen an hour before their date and cancel. Instead, he brought his boys and if she didn't want to go—and who could blame her—he would merely take the boys down to Sammy's Smoke House for burgers and milkshakes and call it a night.

He was dog-tired anyway.

"Why are we stopping, Dad? Milo lives up yonder," Buddy told him.

"Yeah, Papa. I want to see Helen. Aren't we going to see Helen?" Joey wanted to know.

"I like Helen, Daddy," Gavin said. "I promise to be good."

His three boys all sat strapped in the backseat with Joey in the middle. They were dressed in their best jeans, tucked-in pressed shirts and clean sneakers, except for Buddy, who only wore boots. Their hair was combed, their faces scrubbed and their nails were clipped smooth. They were duded up better than he was.

He'd been so concerned about how his boys looked that he hadn't had time to polish himself. Everything he wore was clean and he'd taken a shower, but his clothes weren't his best and his boots had seen better days. Still, he'd had the presence of mind to grab his new straw cream-colored cattleman hat, which at least made him feel as if he was somewhat dressed for the occasion.

Colt turned in his seat. "I'm stopping to make sure you boys know the rules. Can you repeat them for me?"

"No loud talking. No screaming," Gavin said. "Always say please and thank you."

"No going off without asking your permission first," Buddy chimed in. "And no talking when the adults are talking. Even if we have a question?"

"Yes. Wait until there's a break in the conversation."

Buddy nodded.

Colt looked at Joey, who hadn't said anything. "What else?"

Joey shrugged.

"What's the matter?"

"I don't feel so good."

Colt cringed. Joey had been sluggish all day, but Colt assumed Joey was simply tired. "I need specifics, remember?"

"My head hurts."

Colt reached over and touched Joey's face and, sure enough, he felt hot. "You have a fever, son. Probably getting a cold. I'm sorry, but we need to take care of this."

Tears instantly streamed down Joey's cheeks. "But I don't want to go home, Papa. I want to see Helen. I want a milkshake."

"I know, but you need to rest to get that fever down."

"I don't want to go to bed. It's too early. It's still daytime." The sun had just slipped behind the mountains.

"We'll figure it out. I promise."

But Joey couldn't stop crying.

The first thing Colt had to do was cancel the date with Helen, and he didn't want to do it on the phone. Seeing as how he was only a block away, he decided to drive to her house and tell her in person. It seemed as if he and Helen would never get the time they needed to talk.

"I'm sorry, son," Colt said as he drove the block to Helen's house, parked the SUV and got out. "I'll only be a minute, but I promise we'll stop and get you that milkshake, Joey. We'll see Helen another time."

Joey nodded, and wiped his tears from his face. His cheeks were turning a bright red. Colt knew he needed to make his excuses and get his son back home quickly.

When he walked closer to the front door he noticed it was open, which meant she was inside doing something. He'd known Helen for quite some time, and whenever he stopped by to an open door it meant that he should make himself at home while he waited for her, only this time he couldn't wait.

He stepped inside. "Helen, are you here? My boy's sick and I have to…"

But he stopped dead silent when he saw Helen descending the stairs wearing a long floral dress, heels and a deep pink shawl over her shoulders. She didn't say a word, but from the way she was dressed—combined with the warm smile on her face—he knew whatever she wanted to tell him about had to be serious. They had a connection, he and Helen, and he had no intention of ignoring it, despite the fact that she was carrying someone else's child.

He'd only seen Helen in a dress maybe a handful of times, and two of those times were at funerals. She looked positively glowing. He'd sometimes forget what a true knockout she was and the vision of her descending those steps left him muddleheaded and confused.

"I hope I didn't keep you waiting too long," she said as she glided toward him.

Colt couldn't move or speak. He felt about as useless as a four-card flush until Buddy's voice brought him back to reality.

"Dad, Joey just puked all over the backseat."

AN HOUR LATER, Joey was cleaned up and dosed with the children's medication that Colt had picked up at Angie's

Pharmacy after he'd called the doctor to describe Joey's symptoms. The doctor would stop by Colt's house in the morning to check on Joey, but until then the medication brought down his fever and settled his stomach. He was now resting in Milo's recliner. He looked so tiny and innocent in the massive chair all snuggled up with a thick blanket, head nestled on a pillow and his blond curly hair tousled around his sweet face. Anybody looking at him would never know what a handful he could be.

The cheese pizza Helen ordered for her and the boys, along with a pizza with everything on it for Colt, had arrived and she arranged the fast-food blitz along with plates, milk and napkins on the double-wide coffee table in the living room. She'd also mixed up a batch of hot cocoa with tiny marshmallows, the cup rimmed in chocolate syrup she figured the boys would love. At first they'd all wanted milkshakes, but when she described her hot cocoa, there was no contest.

She'd changed out of her fancy dress and slipped back into comfortable jeans and a loose-fitting maternity tee, pulled a couple beers out of the fridge for Colt, downloaded a movie for the boys and intended to spend the entire night on the sofa snuggling with Colt's boys. A vision she'd always thought would be impossible. She had the notion that his boys never relaxed for one minute. It was comforting to know they had a downtime.

She felt peaceful. Her stomach seemed to like cheese pizza and her heart enjoyed having Colt nearby.

"I'm really sorry about all of this," he whispered for about the hundredth time. "This isn't what I'd planned."

Colt sat at the end of the sofa next to the chair she was in, surrounded by pillows and blankets. Gavin sat with her in the oversize chair, while Buddy was stretched out on the sofa with his head resting on Colt's lap. It felt as natural as when she rode Tater in competition, and it made her wonder if she could ever settle for a more sedate lifestyle.

A lifestyle of evening movies, pizza and Colt Granger. She gazed over at him as he watched the movie. That chiseled face of his, his sun-streaked hair that looked like silk as it skimmed the back of his shirt collar, those broad shoulders and knowing how good he made her feel caused her to want to take him to her bed all over again.

Her baby kicked, throwing her out of her romantic trance. The reality of living with Colt Granger was sprawled out around her in the form of three little rascals. No way could she ever handle his boys nor did she think she could ever truly love Colt. The man was a dyed-in-the-wool rancher. Tied to a stationary lifestyle whereas she was a free spirit who loved the circuit, loved to compete and loved her freedom.

She knew parts of that vision would have to change because of the baby, but taking on more than her one child was simply out of the question. She could see herself doing more nights like this after the baby was born. Anything more and she'd feel confined. No, she and Colt would share custody, and the boys would have another sibling, but that was as far as she wanted it to go.

"Don't worry about it," Helen told him. "It's fun spending time with you and your boys, especially when we're not all running after piglets at the fair."

He chuckled. "I'll second that."

"This is the good part," Gavin said. "We have to be really quiet so we can hear it."

"I'm sorry, sweetie," Helen whispered. "We'll be quiet so you can hear."

"Thanks," he said, as polite as pie.

Gavin took after his grandpa, Dodge. When either of

them wanted another person to do something or clarify a truth or a task they had a respectful way of asking that made the person want to cooperate. They found ways to gently let the person know their wishes without being heavy-handed.

Helen was nothing like that, which was probably a failing on her part, especially in her situation. She wanted to blurt out her news. Tell Colt this was his child, and let it go at that. She didn't need anything more than him just being there for her and the baby, being a good dad, which she knew he already was, and helping out financially whenever their baby needed it.

She blew out air knowing sure as rain her ideas of parenthood and his were going to be the exact opposite. Still, she realized she had to take Milo's advice and break it to him gently, so to speak, without dropping it like a ton of bricks.

Of course, that information wouldn't be coming out tonight with the boys so close by. Once again she'd have to wait until a more appropriate moment. Which made her wonder if that appropriate moment would ever be right. Could she possibly go her entire pregnancy without telling him? Was that even remotely possible?

No, she had to tell him. Tonight. She would ask him to follow her into the kitchen and she'd tell him while they stood under the elk antlers that hung over the doorway. She'd be up front and lay it out there as if it was just another fact of life.

First she'd tell him about his hat, which she noticed as soon as he walked in. And yes, it was a great hat, cream-colored, that sat on his head just perfectly and made his eyes look even bluer than they were naturally.

She screwed up her courage, turned to Colt, took a deep breath, thought about how to open the conversation by telling him about his great hat, when Buddy suddenly looked at them.

"Are you going to move back to Briggs with your new sheep herder husband once your baby cooks? If you do, can we come over for more nights like this? You make the best hot chocolate ever!"

Buddy never did share that gentle persuasion trait. Unfortunately, he was more like Helen.

Colt nearly choked on his beer, while Helen didn't move or blink—more of the deer in the headlights phenomenon.

"I…um…" she finally said, but couldn't quite finish her thought.

"Buddy, what kind of… You… Huh? That makes no sense." Colt shifted forward, struggling for words.

Buddy's forehead furrowed.

Gavin chimed in. "But, Daddy, Nathan Haug told us his older sister told him that Helen's got a baby in the oven and a reluctant husband on the lamb. Nathan can't tell a lie or his mom will wash his mouth out with girlie soap and he hates the taste of girlie soap."

The music from the movie pulsed in Helen's ears. It seemed dark and ominous. Just what she didn't need.

"Well, I…" She couldn't seem to form the right words.

That was the problem; she didn't know what words to form. Never in a million years did she think Colt's boys would put it all out on the table.

"You boys shouldn't be listening to such things. That's gossip and gossip is usually a tangle of misconceptions. Now watch your movie. Helen did a lot for us tonight and we don't want to be rude by asking her a lot of questions."

"I didn't mean to be rude," Buddy said. "I just wanted to know if we could still come over."

"What are you going to name your baby?" Gavin wanted to know.

Suddenly Joey was awake, rubbing his eyes and asking his own questions. "When will it be ready to come out of the oven? I like babies. They're funny."

"Now you boys just settle down." He turned to Helen, a great big smile on his face. "This town sure does like to stir things up. You better set these boys straight before they spread their own tales about your baby."

"Sounds as if they need a crash course on where babies come from first," Helen said.

"They've seen enough calves get born on the ranch to know babies don't bake in ovens," Colt said, giving his boys a fatherly look.

"That's what I told Nathan, but he said a mother's belly is like an oven and when the baby's cooked it pops out."

"That's not exactly how it works," Colt said, sliding to the edge of the sofa, looking uncomfortable with the discussion.

"Well, then, how does it work?" Gavin asked, his little face filled with anticipation.

Colt's eyes widened as he turned toward Helen, obviously seeking help in the matter.

She grinned, glad the weight of the moment had fallen on Colt's shoulders and not hers. "Don't look at me," she told him. "I'm just an oven."

Chapter Four

On the road home from spending the evening with Helen, Colt had tried his best to explain to his boys where babies actually came from. He stopped and started so many times though, eventually, Joey fell asleep again, Gavin plugged in his earbuds to listen to a story on his e-reader and Buddy lost interest. All in all, Colt was glad he'd gotten through that night without it being a complete catastrophe.

Now as he and his boys made their way up to his dad's front porch for Sunday dinner, his mind churned with unanswered questions about Helen.

He still didn't know what she had wanted to talk to him about, but figured it must have something to do with her baby, maybe about the father and her plans for the future. Whatever the topic, he had to admit it felt good just being around her again. She was like a cool drink of water on a hot day, and he wished he could spend more evenings drinking her in. Colt liked having her in town. She had a calming effect on him and his boys that he liked and they needed. Plus, he still couldn't get their lovemaking out of his head. Maybe it was wrong of him, seeing as how she was pregnant with another man's baby, but where the heck was that other man? Did the guy even know she was carrying his child? And what happened between them to make her move in with her parents?

What he didn't understand was how she could have made love to him when she was also fooling around with some other dude. That kind of rash behavior wasn't something he would have expected of her and it made him about as sorrowful as a bloodhound that lost its trail.

The more Colt was reminded of her, the more questions popped up unanswered. He knew this was all Helen's business and not his, but dang it all if he wasn't falling for her when clear thinking told him to back away.

He decided he needed to do exactly that…back away, before he couldn't help himself. Not only would he for sure get his heart broken when the child's daddy came back into the picture, but he had a deep fear of dangerous complications during a pregnancy. Consciously he knew this was an overreaction to his wife's passing soon after Joey was born. Nevertheless, he couldn't live with it if he allowed Helen to capture his heart only to lose her if her pregnancy took a fatal turn.

On several levels, allowing himself to fall for Helen was like grabbing the branding iron on the wrong end.

Colt donned his best happy face as he stared down at his boys. Joey was feeling much better after sleeping for most of Saturday, and it seemed as though his brothers didn't catch whatever cold bug he'd been suffering from. Plus, Colt had been putting in a lot of hours on the ranch and neglecting his boys, so he wanted to make it up to them.

"If you boys behave tonight, I'll take you out to play some video games after dinner."

Colt usually didn't believe in bribing his boys, but these were desperate times.

"We'll be good, Daddy. We promise," Gavin said.

"Yeah, we won't even laugh if you don't want us to," Joey added.

"It's not about laughing. It's about causing a fuss."

"Good thing Gramps doesn't have any baby piggies or we might never get to play a video game again for as long as we live," Joey said.

"You sure got that right, little man," Colt said as he picked up Joey and gave him a twirl. Then he held him upside down as he walked up the front porch stairs, all the while Joey couldn't stop laughing. His other two boys tickled Joey's belly. Complete chaos ensued as they all stumbled up the stairs.

The redwood log house was big, and old, and needed work, but Colt and his brothers wouldn't trade it for a castle. This was their home, their heritage, their land, and nothing would ever change that.

Buddy opened the front door and Colt and his boys tumbled inside, making more noise than a herd of cattle. Joey let out one of his sweet belly laughs and Colt couldn't help but laugh out loud along with him. Colt put Joey down and closed the door just as Scout, his brother Blake's six-year-old daughter, came running over to join in on the laughter. She wore her usual jeans, a pink T-shirt and her latest pair of red cowgirl boots. The big difference in Scout was that ever since Blake had married Maggie, Scout was more little girl than little tomboy. She had taken on more boy traits than girl traits soon after Blake split with his wife and she moved to L.A. Blake hadn't known how to handle a little girl. After all, he was surrounded by boys, but Maggie knew exactly what to do. Now Scout seemed to be the perfect blend. She could stand up to her male cousins with bows in her hair and bright pink polish on her fingernails. "We've got company again tonight," she said, looking all proud of herself for being the first to announce it. "And she brought homemade pie and ice cream. You want to see the pie? She's making it warm in the oven."

She took Joey's hand and the two of them ran toward the kitchen. Gavin and Buddy followed close behind.

Colt's apprehension heightened. He guessed one of his brother's must've fixed him up with yet another woman…a woman who could bake.

"About time you showed up," Dodge said as Colt ambled toward the long wooden table that was already set with their mom's mustard-colored Fiesta ware. Mom had passed when he and Travis were still in their teens, but Dodge liked to set the table on Sundays exactly like she had when she was alive.

Sunday dinner always featured some type of potato from their most recent crop. No other potato but their own was ever allowed in the main Granger house. Dodge had laid down that law years ago and it stuck. This harvest would produce their first crop of Fingerlings, including Purple Peruvian. Colt had also put in a few acres of Yukon Golds and Gems. He had to argue with Dodge for those crops. Dodge believed in exclusively growing Russets, but, after much debate, Colt had convinced him to try other types of potatoes. Harvest had already begun on some of those crops and so far they looked good, but Dodge was still skeptical about Colt's "experiment," as he liked to call it, and only served up pure Russet potatoes in his house.

"Dinner's almost ready. Take your seats," Dodge ordered as he set a large platter of scalloped potatoes on the table next to a rack of perfectly cooked lamb. Colt's boys, Scout and the two ranch dogs, siblings Suzie and Mush, part wolf with other parts unknown, hustled together in a great stampede of miniature cowboy boots and heavy paws, pounding across the wooden floor toward the table.

"Glad you could make it," Blake told Colt. "If I didn't know better, I'd say you've been avoiding us."

This was the first Sunday in two weeks that Colt had made it over for dinner. His boys never missed a Sunday because most of the time they'd been hanging around at Dodge's house, but Colt had been way too busy with the harvest and ranch duties to make it over for dinner. Truth be told, he purposely stayed away knowing full well what his brothers were up to, and tonight seemed to be no exception.

"Just be glad Colt's here," Maggie said, looking like the country girl Blake had known was hidden behind her city swagger. Ever since she'd become a member of the family, she'd taken to ranch life. Her black hair was usually pulled back into an easy ponytail, makeup on that pretty face seemed almost nonexistent and her bright blue eyes always sparkled whenever she looked at her man.

"Thanks, Maggie. Been busy, is all," Colt lied, kind of. "Might get a call during dinner and have to run out."

Colt was thinking dinner could get real uncomfortable and he might need an exit plan.

"If you're that busy maybe we need to hire more help," Travis said.

That was Travis, always thinking of ways to make Colt's life easier…one hired hand or one woman at a time.

"Been thinking about doing just that, but in the meantime I may have to—"

"Ain't nobody runnin' nowhere during this here dinner," Dodge stated, looking directly at Colt. "Ain't nothing more important than family, and you, son, need to be spending more time in the bosom of yours."

The kids giggled as Dodge took his seat at the head of the table. He waved his hands toward his grandchildren to get their attention. "Now, now, settle down. You kids don't want our company thinking we're a rowdy bunch."

The boys suppressed their giggles, with Scout holding her hand over her mouth to stop the laughter from pouring out.

"No need for me to hire more people," Colt said to Travis. "I've got everything under control."

Colt heard the oven door slam shut in the kitchen and he sat up straighter. Shoot. He'd temporarily forgotten about his brothers' latest candidate for the "perfect fit."

"Seems to me control is something that's eluding you, son, in more ways than just this here land," Dodge said.

Colt felt as if he'd been hog-tied into some sort of family tough-love night, instead of just Sunday dinner. His dad sometimes rode him about his lack of discipline with his boys, and any second now a pretty blonde or brunette would stroll out of the kitchen with a homemade pie she'd just taken out of the oven to prove to Colt she could cook—a trait his brothers thought might be important to him, considering the mother of his children had been a fantastic cook.

On the other hand, Helen could barely boil water.

"You boys stop picking on Colt or I'm going to pack up my apple pie and take it back home with me," Mrs. Abernathy said as she walked out of the kitchen carrying a pie between two hot pads.

The girl in the kitchen was retired nurse Edith Abernathy? Colt didn't understand.

She set the pie on the table, took the seat that was next to Dodge, and everyone bowed their head for a prayer, ignoring her presence as if this was as normal as lemonade on a hot day.

When the prayer was finished, Colt said, "Nice to see you, Mrs. Abernathy. What brings you out today?"

"This is her third Sunday dinner with us, son," Dodge said, speaking for Mrs. Abernathy. "Had you come 'round the last two weeks you would've known she's now a permanent fixture on Sunday."

"Yeah, and she brings us the best pies ever," Scout announced. "Today we have an apple pie with ice cream. Doesn't it look yummy? I helped her make it."

Mrs. Edith Abernathy was a feisty woman somewhere in her early seventies who spoke her mind despite what her obstinate mind might conjure up. She had an elusive early history that no one could quite pin down that eventually led to her becoming a registered nurse. Colt knew Dodge had taken a liking to her ever since she'd helped out with Kitty's babies. Kitty was Maggie's sister and the reason why Maggie had come to Briggs in the first place. What Colt hadn't realized was exactly when and how Edith had become a permanent fixture at their Sunday dinner table.

From the way Dodge looked over at her as if she was as sweet as barnyard milk, he figured there was more to this woman than just a dinner guest.

"Am I to guess that you and Edith are an item now?" Colt blurted out. He really didn't know where that came from. He was usually the son who skirted the obvious, but lately, skirting the obvious wasn't working so well for him.

Everyone stopped talking. The food dishes that were being passed around stopped moving. Forks stood at the ready. Even Suzie crawled out from under the table to give Dodge a little *ruff*.

"No guessing about it. I'm courting Edith and anybody who don't much like it can keep their 'pinions to themselves." Dodge liked to ward off any grief headed his way by making sure everyone knew where he stood on the matter.

Colt grinned at his dad. "No dissent here. I think it's great."

With that said, the food continued to be passed around the table and empty plates were filled with potatoes, slices of lamb, salad and homemade mint jelly that Dodge put up himself.

For the rest of the meal, Colt watched as his dad and Edith made eye contact as if they were sharing a secret. He hadn't seen his dad so happy in years.

Colt, on the other hand, hadn't felt that kind of happiness for longer than he'd like to admit. Although he loved his boys more than his next breath, he longed for a woman by his side.

Reason told him that woman couldn't be Helen, but pure stubbornness told him he couldn't give up on her just yet.

HELEN HADN'T WANTED to go out that Sunday night, but Milo had insisted. And of all places, Pia's Pizza Parlor had been his restaurant of choice. Not that she was complaining, cheese pizza was her survival food, and Pia's Pizza was her favorite. Her only concern was that it was a kids' restaurant, complete with video games and a trampoline room; a safe haven for weary parents who needed a break from their little darlings. And if she didn't already know that Sunday was family night at the Granger ranch, she wouldn't have agreed to come. Pia's Pizza was not the place to spill her situation to Colt—

way too much kid chaos. She had wanted to come clean on Friday, but once again, the timing wasn't right.

So instead, she remained a scandalous source of gossip for the entire town of Briggs.

She wished she could tap her heels together and be back home in Jackson, with her stepmom bringing her hot tea, her cousins all around her cracking jokes, the occasional friend dropping in to see how she was doing and her dad talking savings accounts.

But there was no rest for the weary, as her mom used to say, and yes, was she ever weary. However, on the brighter side, Pia's Pizza was loud, overrun with parents and squabbling siblings and the perfect place for Helen to lose herself for an hour or two. She had ordered a medium cheese pizza and a root beer float, while Milo had ordered an extra-large Pia Pizza with everything on it including double anchovies.

Amanda Fittswater, Milo's "friend," had come along and convinced two-hundred-and-seventy-five-pound Milo to join her in the trampoline room. Helen could only imagine what that must look like after she saw most of the kids come running out.

"Milo can sure clear out a room," Colt's voice echoed somewhere behind her as she licked the straw clean of ice cream from her float. She was sucking up the last of it, and thinking that she might need another one, when Colt jolted her out of her sugar bliss.

He came around to her side of the table looking better than a man had a right to. "Mind if I join you?"

She wondered if Milo knew he'd be there. If he and Colt had it all planned.

He was alone, but she knew his boys were somewhere close. "Colt. Hi. Sure, grab a seat. But shouldn't you be at your dad's place, enjoying a home-cooked meal?"

"Already did that. Been bringing the boys here after dinner so they can run off some steam before their school week starts."

She figured as much. Milo was even craftier than she gave him credit for.

"How's that working out for you?"

He shrugged. "I'm still hopeful."

Then he took the seat across from her, and goose bumps prickled her skin.

She, Milo and Amanda had been seated at the end of a long table that sat twelve. The family of six that had been sitting at the far end had just left.

They were alone in the crowd.

He handed her a napkin, grinning. "You never could feel ice cream on your chin. I remember that from when we were in first grade together."

She grabbed the napkin, completely embarrassed, and wiped her chin. "You used to tease me for it in front of everybody."

"Things change. Now I think it's cute."

She chuckled. "It's only because you're used to messy faces on your boys."

"Big difference. On you it's sexy. On them it's a mess."

She'd never heard him call her sexy before and she liked it. "Why, Colt Granger, are you flirting with me?" She batted her eyes.

His face went pink as a wide smile creased his lips as he leaned in closer, his elbows on the table, chin resting on one hand. "I believe I am, yes."

"I like it."

"Me, too."

Then they both started talking at the same time.

"I need to…" she said.

"I decided that…" he said.

They laughed. It seemed as though they'd been so uptight with each other ever since she'd come home, that laughing was something they'd forgotten how to do.

"Ladies first," he insisted, tipping his new hat to her, sliding back in his chair.

But she didn't want that gentleman's option. "Thanks, but I'd like you to go first this time. Please."

He took a deep breath, and began. "Okay. Here's what I'm thinking. I think it's important for you to know that I'm here if you need me. You don't have to tell me anything about the child's daddy, or why you're not with him, or even if you're going to raise the baby yourself or let somebody else raise it as their own. Whatever you decide is your business, but I'm here to give you all the help you need."

She knew it was difficult for Colt to tell her these things and she appreciated his honesty. "Thanks. That's really generous of you, Colt."

He reached over and laid his hand on top of hers. She instantly felt warm and safe. As if all she needed was his reassurance that everything was going to be all right and she could face whatever came her way.

"Just tell me what you need, and I'll make it happen."

"Anything?"

He blew out a sigh, looking all serious, as if he was ready to pull down the moon if she asked. "Yes, anything."

She picked up her empty glass and handed it to him. "More, please. Another root beer float."

"This isn't exactly what I had in mind."

"It's a good start."

He grinned and his eyes glistened with that same sly little sparkle they'd had right before they'd jumped into bed together. Immediately a spark shot through her and if they weren't in a public place with kids and people everywhere, it would have been difficult for her not to want a repeat performance.

Fortunately, the laughter and noise combined with the music in the restaurant suddenly escalated and reality came rushing back at her.

"I'll be right back," he told her then made his way to the soda bar, where she could see him ordering her another one.

While she watched him, she scolded herself for even thinking such thoughts. He wasn't the guy for her and never would be. Sure he was cute, and sure she liked him, and okay, he was a great lover, but she wasn't now nor had she ever been in love with him, even if his eyes did sparkle when he laughed.

When he turned back to her holding an overflowing mug of soda and ice cream, several napkins, and trying desperately not to let it drip all over the floor and him, all the while smiling at her, she felt her face flush with heat.

She figured it had to be a hot flash of some sort because of the baby.

Nothing more.

She took a deep breath and slowly let it out, trying to restore her sanity, her reason. But the man had a charisma that got under her skin. And watching him walk toward her, smiling, carrying over her favorite treat, only made it worse.

She forced herself to look away for a moment and regain her composure.

When he finally arrived at the table, and plunked the mug down on a bundle of napkins in front of her, the words simply poured out of her. "Colt, there's more to this baby than you think."

She ran her hands over her belly, and cupped the underside. Her baby moved inside her.

"He just kicked. Do you want to feel him?"

The noise level in the place suddenly rose.

"You know it's a boy?" Colt was almost yelling now.

"Here, put your hand here." He reached for the spot, and she placed her hand on top of his. As soon as she did, a warm, silky feeling ran through her.

She pulled her hand away just as her baby gave her another strong kick.

"He sure feels sturdy."

Then, as if someone turned a switch, Colt pulled his hand away and stuck it into his jean pocket. He instantly sat down, and gazed out at the crowd, clearing his throat.

Odd behavior from a man with three children of his own. Almost as if he was uncomfortable with the situation.

Helen didn't know what to make of it, but she pressed on with what she knew she had to say. "I don't know for sure if it's a boy, but I have a strong feeling a girl isn't in your gene pool. Colt, this baby is yours."

He leaned in, cupping his right ear. The noise level had dramatically increased. "Sorry, I didn't catch that. What did you say about my sons?"

"I said, I'm carrying your son." She was shouting now.

Colt shook his head. "This is crazy. I can't hear you at all anymore."

A siren echoed off in the distance as Joey came running up to their table. "Papa! Papa! Come quick. Gavin and another kid are caught in the stuffed animal machine."

Colt stood. "What? Gavin? No. I warned you boys…"

Joey grabbed his hand and pulled. "You gotta get

them out before the kid eats all the stuffed animals. He's got two in his mouth right now. Hurry, Papa!"

The sirens stopped just as two firemen carrying axes rushed into the restaurant. The taller of the two nodded toward Colt. "Don't worry. We'll get your boy free."

"Excuse me, Helen, but…" Colt and Joey followed right behind the firemen, while Helen remained frozen at the table.

As everyone in the restaurant rushed toward the stuffed animal machine, Helen burst into great big, uncontrollable sobs.

It finally hit her: this was her new life. From now on, she was doomed to being friends with the men and women of the local fire department, destined to having her child caught in claw machines and generally wreaking havoc along with his brothers everywhere they went.

She knew her pregnancy caused her to cry for almost any reason, good or bad, but lately simply being around Colt's family brought on the waterworks. She supposed it was worry that her sweet unborn child was fated to be a hell-raiser exactly like the rest of Colt's boys and she had no idea how she would handle it.

That thought nearly paralyzed her. She never wanted one child, let alone be connected to three more. All she ever desired since she was a teen was to win the national cowboy mounted shooting championship. Then, if she worked really hard, to go on to win the world championship. She didn't think she would ever be able to settle down and even if she couldn't compete anymore she planned on opening her own riding school. Some of her best memories were from M & M Riding School and she'd like to make that happen for her own students, someday.

She always saw herself as her own person, making

her own decisions. How on earth would she ever learn to handle anything less? It wasn't as if she could depend on Colt to take care of their baby while she was on the road. All he ever did was work on the Granger ranch. She knew this to be true from the few years she'd been living in Briggs. He was hardly ever home, occasionally disciplined his boys and barely took the time to show them the elements of right and wrong. Dodge was more of a father to them than Colt, or at least that was the impression she always had. Ever since his wife passed, those boys of his ran wild. Everybody knew it, and everybody tried to stay out of their way.

Including her.

She cried harder as another team of firemen ran past her and she realized that getting Colt alone long enough for a private conversation was next to impossible, and that the chance of them ever making love again, even if she wanted to, was about as probable as her carrying a baby girl.

BRIGHT AND EARLY on Monday morning, Colt drove his pickup slowly by the buildings that made up the M & M Riding School, liking what he saw. Dodge had asked him to check it out when he heard it was on the market. Colt had been dragging his feet about taking a look, but Dodge thought it would be perfect. Colt thought it would take too much work.

There were some things he and his dad simply could not agree on.

Fortunately, so far, Colt had to admit, Dodge might be right on this one.

He parked in the small lot, got out and walked toward the main house under a warm sun as the soft breezes coming off the mountains slid across his face. He secured his hat on his head, in case one of those breezes got a little rough. Yes, this piece of land would initially cost a bit more. They'd have to tear down most of the buildings, but the land already had water, natural gas, electricity and septic, and wasn't far from the main road. The money they'd save on those four essentials alone would save the consortium a bundle in the long run. The other parcels were still raw and needed to be developed. The time and cost could be staggering, whereas this parcel looked about as perfect as red paint on a barn.

He wished Travis had come with him to see this, but he'd been busy in town at Dream Weaver Inn repairing a porch. Travis spent a lot of time at the Inn helping out the owner, Nick Biondi, whenever he could. Nick was like a second dad to Travis, so doing carpentry work around the Inn was something Travis enjoyed. Besides, Travis had always had a soft spot for Nick's estranged daughter, Bella, the one girl Travis might actually settle down for. However, she lived and worked in Chicago, and the chances of her ever returning to Briggs were next to nil.

Colt would have to decide on which property and write up the proposal on his own this time. At least he knew Dodge would be happy, but as far as the two other families in the consortium, he'd have to give them some hard numbers.

He planned on spending the rest of the day doing the research on the cost comparison. Two of his boys were in school at the moment, while Joey spent the day with Dodge. So far this year Buddy and Gavin had managed to keep out of trouble with their teachers. But after last night's fiasco at the pizza parlor, Colt was losing his confidence in his ability to raise them alone. His brothers were right. They needed a mom to help discipline them. He had a hard time in that department. Buddy still woke up in the middle of the night calling his mom's name. Granted, it wasn't very often anymore, but it still happened. Gavin was a loose cannon most of the time, and Joey acted as if somebody stole his rudder.

It was a good thing no one had gotten hurt the previous night. As it turned out, the two firemen were able to dismantle the back of the machine and release the toddler and Gavin within minutes.

The toddler's parents, both high school classmates of Colt's, had scooped up their daughter and given Colt a look that told him they were trying to keep the lid on their can of cuss words. Just as well, 'cause Colt never did take a liking to either one of them and may have said something that he might be regretting this morning.

The riding school was all but abandoned now. There were a few people over by the stables, probably tending to their horses until they could move them, and a rented moving truck sat in front of the main house.

As he walked by the barn, thinking he might keep the big old red barn for storage, a sniffling sound stopped him in his tracks. At first he couldn't make it out. Then as he came closer, he knew it was the distinctive sound of a woman crying.

He hustled around the side of the barn, then to the front entrance, and there, perched on a bale of hay, sat Helen, head resting on her knees, face buried in her arms, crying her eyes out. Tater was tied to the old ornate iron post just outside the barn door that had held countless horses before him.

Colt approached steady and easylike, not wanting to scare either one of them. Tater blew out air and whinnied at his approach, which caused Helen to look up.

"Hey," Colt cooed, soft and steadylike. "Whatever

it is that's causing you so much heartache, I'm here to help."

He sat down next to her on the hay, handed her the clean white handkerchief that he always kept in his shirt pocket, then rubbed her back. Her floral perfume wafted around him and he moved in closer. She smelled like spring, like everything brand-new, like clean sheets... Or was that just wishful thinking?

When she looked up at him, her eyes puffy from weeping, her cheeks wet with tears, he wanted nothing more than to fix whatever it was that had made her so upset.

She hiccuped, drew in a ragged breath, wiped her eyes and squeezed her wet nose with his handkerchief.

"Oh, Colt, this place is so sad. Everybody's gone. The school is almost abandoned and I feel as if I lost my best friend. I loved it here, loved my teachers, loved the friends I made, loved the Miltons. They already moved to town. Did you know that? The only people still working here are the caretakers, and they leave the end of the month. I don't know what I expected, but I didn't expect to see the place so...abandoned. I mean I knew they were retiring, but I didn't think it was happening so fast. At least not like this."

She blew her nose and rested her head on his shoulder. He liked being able to comfort her. Helen wasn't the kind of woman who needed much comforting, so this felt good. Made him feel as if he was making a difference.

"Sweetheart, the school itself has been closed for almost a year."

"It has?"

He nodded and she sobbed into his handkerchief. "How did I not know this? I was just here a few months ago when I left Tater with them, and no one said a word to me about the school closing. I always hear about if someone in town gets a new puppy, or has a new girl-friend or boyfriend, but nobody told me that the school closed?" She looked at him, sniffling. "Did one of the Miltons get sick or something?"

He slid a thick strand of her silky red hair off her wet cheek and for a moment was taken by how beautiful she looked, despite her puffy eyes or her tear-soaked face.

So he kissed her. Just a light kiss to tell her he was on her side. She returned the kiss, just as sweet and ten-der as he remembered. Her full lips pressing against his felt warm and inviting, but he knew this couldn't go any further. When they parted and he looked into her sweet, wet eyes, he realized his feelings for her weren't going away anytime soon, despite what reason told him.

She moved back and he immediately stood, upset that he'd allowed the moment to get the best of him. "I, um, I didn't mean for that to happen."

"It's okay, Colt. I enjoyed it." She smiled and Colt felt as if they had a connection. That is until she ran her hand over her baby bump. The father of her baby had a connection to her that could never be broken. Colt knew he was only a good friend, and under the circumstances could never be anything more.

He cleared his tight throat. He went on. "Anyway, the school had fallen on some rough times during the downturn in the economy, so the Miltons decided it was time to let it go. Then last month, they put a down pay-ment on a sweet little bungalow in town and put this place up for sale."

She sat up straighter. "But I thought Mrs. Milton loved this place. Loved the kids and the school."

"She did, but things change. I think it was time to move on, time for a different path for their lives."

Helen stood and walked outside. Colt followed right behind her as she moved up alongside Tater and stroked his head. The horse nuzzled her, letting out a breath, then shifting his front feet.

"I always thought I would eventually run a riding school of my own once I retired from competing. One exactly like this one, but over in Jackson near my family. This place was always the only school around so my dad had to drive me back and forth two or three times a week every summer. In the winter, I'd practice in Jackson. Only in the last couple of years did Jackson get an arena to compare with this one. This arena is still better. I hope someone buys this place and continues on with the school."

He didn't have the nerve to tell her what he wanted to do with the property. With her fragile state of mind, he knew she'd hate him for even thinking of tearing her beloved school down. Instead, he thought he should try a different angle.

"That'll be tough. Even though Briggs is getting back on its feet after the downturn in the economy, finding someone to buy this place and keep it as is will be somewhat of a miracle. I'm thinking the Miltons want a strong buyer, and what that buyer does with the place is up to the new owners. The best thing that can happen to the Miltons is for them to make a nice profit from the sale so they can afford a comfortable retirement without any financial worries."

She turned toward him looking all melancholy. "You're right. They've worked hard all their lives and deserve a break, but still, it would be nice if this place could stay as is. Of course it could use a few repairs. I always thought the main house needed a couple more rooms, and the arena should be enclosed so it could be used all year long. If I was finished competing, and if I had the money, I'd consider buying it. But I'm not ready to settle down yet. I've got a championship or two that I need to win. It's what I've worked my whole life for."

"Sounds as if you never heard that saying—*life is what happens while you're busy making plans.*"

She rubbed her belly. "A baby's not going to stop me from being who I am, Colt. Other women have babies and still compete. With the help of my family, I'll be back on the circuit next year."

"Seems like it might be a lot of work and time shuffling."

"I was never afraid of hard work. My mama taught me that when I was a little girl. She used to say nothing of value ever comes easy. You have to be willing to work hard for the good stuff."

Colt's stomach tightened. What the heck was he doing talking to Helen about riding schools? Giving her ideas? Trying to convince her to settle down? This place was perfect for the storage plant. He certainly didn't need to get into a bidding war with Helen.

"Your mother was a smart woman," he told her, wanting to leave it at that. Helen was a strong-willed woman, and any man who took her on had to be a master at compromise or the two of them would never last a minute.

"Exactly. She also taught me to never be afraid of the truth." She took a deep breath and let it out. "I've got something to say, Colt, and I'm going to come right out and say it."

"It's what I've always admired about you."

She rubbed her belly and stepped toward him. "Colt, this baby, I don't know what you heard, but the truth is—"

"The truth is it's nobody's business but your own."

He didn't know if he was ready to hear about the baby's father. Didn't know if he could take her telling him they were getting married and moving to another state. He didn't know if he could listen to anything about the other man in Helen's life.

But he knew he had no choice.

"And the daddy's," she said. "It's his business, too."

"Certainly, but even then, it depends if he's a good man or not."

The thought had occurred to him that maybe this guy was a real loser and had walked out on Helen, exactly like half the town said.

"Oh, he's a good man. The best, actually. Loving. Smart. He works hard. A good sense of humor. He's an all-around great cowboy."

Colt let out a heavy sigh knowing that any chance he thought he still had with Helen had just gone up in smoke. "Seems to me no more needs to be said."

"Things aren't always what they seem, Colt."

He stared at her, worried now that she was having health issues. That there was something wrong with the baby. His heart raced, his hands shook as he reached out and put his hand on her arm. "Why? Is there something wrong? Are you and the baby okay?"

She took his hand in hers, lacing her fingers through his, but he pulled away. He didn't want her to know how upset he was, didn't want her to feel his tremors.

"I'm fine. Really. And the baby's perfect."

Colt's tension eased up a bit. "Has the dad hurt you in some way?"

She shook her head. "No, Colt. At least not yet."

He tipped his hat farther back on his head, letting his body relax. Helen always was one to be reckoned with. "Now what does that mean exactly?"

She took another deep breath while she slid her foot in the sand making a circle. "Colt, I'm pregnant with your baby. I know it seems impossible, but it's true. The doctor said…"

Hot bile crept up his throat. His stomach clinched and his mouth went dry. He had to stop her from going any further with this crazy talk.

"Wait a minute. Say again?"

"This is your baby, Colt. You're the daddy."

He wanted to get away from her, wanted her to take back what she said. His getting a woman pregnant was next to impossible. No way. "I don't care what the doctor said. The odds are one in a million or something like that. It can't happen."

"Yes, it can and it did. I haven't been with another man, Colt. Just you."

His body tensed again, every muscle tightened. His stomach roiled. Pure emotion overtook him and he spun around as his eyes watered. He instinctively reached for his hankie then remembered he'd given it to Helen. Tears tumbled freely from his eyes as fear gripped his soul. He didn't know how to handle this news, what to do, what to say. It was as if she'd told him he'd hurt someone real bad while he was sleeping, while he was unconscious.

There was no reacting to that information.

No way could he make it right.

He couldn't have gotten her pregnant. Not Helen. He just couldn't have.

"I've got to go," he told her and walked away as tears slid down his face.

Chapter Five

"We need to talk, big brother," Colt told Blake as he stood in his doorway. It was late, a quarter past one in the morning.

"I figured as much when you called," Blake mumbled. He wore a navy sweatshirt and gray pajama bottoms. His sandy-colored hair was a tousled mess, his whiskers looked thick and sleep weathered his eyes.

Colt walked in and sat down on the well-worn tan sofa.

"Can I get you a drink?" Blake offered.

"I think I've already had enough…already."

"I was offering a drink of water."

"Yes. It might help sober me up."

"You already look sober. What's on your mind?"

Blake went off to the kitchen and a couple minutes later, brought back two mugs filled with orange juice. He handed one to Colt then plopped himself down in a leather chair facing his brother.

"I need your advice," Colt said.

"This is a first. Usually, I'm coming to you for advice."

"Things change."

"I should say they do. What's up?"

There was no easy way to say it. "Helen's pregnant with *my* baby."

Saying it out loud made it even more unbelievable. Blake leaned forward. "What?"

"Helen is going to have my baby."

Blake sat back and snickered. "This town comes up with the craziest rumors. I bet you had a good laugh with that one."

Colt stood up and started pacing. "It's not a rumor. It's a fact. She told me herself."

"But didn't you get that feature fixed years ago?"

The rest of the house was dark and quiet. He could hear the grandfather clock ticking in the corner. He always liked that sound. When he was a kid he would sometimes sneak out of his room upstairs and sleep on the sofa just so he could hear it all night long.

"I sure did, but little did I ever think, especially after all this time, that I'd be shootin' real bullets."

Colt walked in circles from the clock, around the sofa then back to the clock, wishing like hell the sound of the clock would work its magic. So far nothing seemed to calm him.

"Sit down. You're making me dizzy."

"I can't. I'm too twitchy."

Blake shifted in his chair. "Wait a minute. You and Helen are…" He made a weird, awkward gesture with his hand.

"One time. We slept together once. It didn't mean anything."

Colt knew it meant more, much more. He hadn't been able to get that night out of his mind, but he never meant for it to lead to another baby, to her getting pregnant. He'd slept with other women since his wife had passed and he'd gotten a vasectomy. Not many, but they hadn't gotten pregnant. Why did Helen have to get pregnant? Helen, a rodeo rat, was the mother to one of his children.

It made him all queasy inside just thinking about it. He took a few gulps of his orange juice with pulp, the way he liked it. It went down hard, and felt like acid in his throat.

"I beg to differ, little brother. It meant a lot. You two made a baby. Do you love her?"

Colt near about choked on that one.

"Helen? Do I love Helen? Me? Her?"

"It's a simple question. Do you love Helen?"

He didn't know how to answer that loaded question. He couldn't be sure of anything at the moment. If Blake had asked him that a couple months ago he would've eagerly said no. They were simply friends with benefits. But lately, every time he'd seen her or talked to her or gotten close enough to smell her perfume, something came over him making him want her in his bed again. Was that love?

It had been so long since he'd actually felt love for a woman that he didn't know.

Still, he did care about her. More than he'd like to admit. But did he love her as in couldn't imagine his life without Helen by his side?

He truly didn't know, and that ambivalence had to mean he didn't.

Or did it?

What he did know was the kiss they shared in the barn stirred up more emotions than a man had a right to feel for such a simple act, almost as if he'd been starving for her affection.

"I can't say that I do, and I can't say that I don't. I rightly don't know what I feel for Helen. She's been my friend for so long that being in love with her never occurred to me. She's not the type of woman I want or more important, what my boys need. Helen can't settle down, can't take root in one place. She loves being on the road too much, loves a competition. Being in love with Helen would be like being in love with the wind."

Blake shook his head. "Seems to me you're making excuses for what's really bothering you about Helen and until you lay it on the table, you and she don't stand a chance."

Colt sat down hard on the sofa, his head hitting the back cushion with such a force it actually hurt. The pain was a good distraction. Raw emotion welled up inside him and he was doing everything he could do to stop it. "I couldn't take it if she died delivering my baby."

Blake went over and sat next to him. "That's what I'm talking about. I knew you were spinning into a dark place. Is she having a difficult pregnancy? Is there something wrong with the baby? Is that why you stopped by tonight?"

Colt stood, not wanting to display his emotions. "As far as I know everything's good. At least that's what she told me. I know it's crazy to think she could die, but dammit all, I can't help myself. I couldn't take it if anything happened to Helen or the baby."

"You're jumping the gun here, brother. You're letting the past take hold of your future. Helen's not your boys' mom," Blake told him. "Helen's a healthy young woman. Besides, the woman shoots guns while riding horseback. I wouldn't count her out just yet. When did she tell you?"

"This afternoon."

"And what supportive, loving words did you say after she told you?"

He was embarrassed to admit to his bad behavior.

"That's just it. I didn't say anything. I walked away."

Blake stood and put his arm around Colt's shoulder. "I may not know much about women, but I do know that wasn't what she needed."

"I know. She probably hates me."

"Hate's not strong enough. The way I see it, you've got to do the right thing."

"Like ask her to marry me?"

"Slow down there, little brother. Maybe you should start by apologizing for being such a horse's butt. That might get you back on speaking terms."

Colt headed for the door, wanting to drive directly over to Milo's house. Blake stopped him. "You're not going anywhere in the shape you're in. Get some sleep and go over there when you're feeling more confident."

"Right. Sleep. I could use some sleep."

"It will all look better in the morning."

"The morning."

Suddenly the tension Colt had been carrying around began to drain from his every pore. He felt so tired he couldn't keep his eyes open.

"Mrs. Abernathy sitting with your boys tonight?" Blake asked.

"She sure is."

"Then you're staying right here tonight. That guest room has your name on it."

As soon as Blake suggested it, Colt staggered in the direction of the bedroom, pulling his boots off as he went and dropping onto the queen-size bed before Blake could say good-night.

"I'm such a fool," he mumbled right before he fell into a deep sleep.

"I STILL CAN'T believe he walked away from you," Milo said as he and Helen ambled into Belly Up Saloon on Main Street in downtown Briggs. Milo couldn't seem to let it go, and although Helen was completely heartbroken over Colt's response, especially after that kiss they shared, at least now she knew where she stood.

She'd come to Briggs specifically to tell Colt about their baby and to move Tater into Milo's stable until she could find a more permanent home for him in Jackson, both of which she could now say she'd accomplished. With those two tasks completed, she was ready to return to her parents' house in the morning. She had less than eight weeks left before her due date and it was about time she started preparing for her baby's arrival... Apparently without Colt Granger.

"I know, it's not what you expected," she said as they stepped into the noisy bar. "It's not what I expected, either, but it is what it is."

"That don't make it right."

Milo secured his chocolate-colored sloped pinchfront hat on his head as they momentarily stood next to the door surveying the room. Milo didn't consider himself dressed for the outdoors without his favorite hat perched easy on his head. He wore a black-and-red-plaid flannel shirt, jeans and black cowboy boots—an outfit he felt the most comfortable in, though lately he'd added a couple blue-checked shirts, courtesy of Amanda's influence, no doubt.

He was on his way to Spud Drive-In for the last double feature of the season. The drive-in always closed for the season in late September, so Milo's part-time job was coming to an end, which normally meant he'd be hanging around the house all winter. But this winter, he'd taken a part-time bartending job at Belly Up

Saloon. He was getting a quick rundown of the place from the owner, while Helen was staying to visit with some of her friends.

As soon as she'd walked through the heavy glass door, she felt as if she was coming home. Familiar faces were everywhere, all smiling and glad to see her. The steady beat of country music bounced off of every table, chair, picture and wall. She hadn't been in the place since she'd been in town and for the life of her, she couldn't figure out why.

She loved this honky-tonk and all the people who patronized it. She loved the bare wooden planks on the floor and the mirrored mahogany bar that extended the entire length of the west wall. She loved the ambience and the smell of beer but most of all she loved how special she felt walking through the crowd. Everyone seemed to want to give her a hug or a warm hello. It made her feel truly welcomed.

"Well, at least he didn't tell me to never talk to him before he walked away. It was bad enough seeing the M & M Riding School virtually abandoned and up for sale. I always thought I'd be able to buy it or maybe a place just like it when I retired from the circuit. I wish the Miltons had waited a few years. I'm not ready to settle down yet, not that I could afford the place if I was. But it doesn't matter, I still want that world championship win."

"Does Colt know how you feel about that school?"

"Sure. I told him, but what does that have to do with anything? That's my dream, not his. Besides, he doesn't want to have anything to do with me or our baby. That's pretty clear now."

The words still hurt when she said them out loud, but she held back the tears.

"You want I should drive over to his place and talk to that boy? Knock a little sense into him?"

"No, but thanks for the offer. He has to come around on his own…or not. Either way, I don't hate him. It's not what either of us expected. If I know Colt, he's probably trying to figure what to do next."

Helen had been all set to spend the night on the sofa in Milo's living room surrounded by an evening's worth of comfort foods: a bowl of green olives, buttery popcorn, a generous slice of peanut butter and chocolate cheese-cake, an entire cheese pizza, raw carrots and a tall glass of whole milk. She tried to include at least one raw vegetable and one glass of milk with every meal. She'd even slipped into her favorite flannel pajamas, the deep pink ones with kitschy-looking cowgirls riding bucking broncos or sitting on wooden fences, a present from Sarah, her teammate, two birthdays ago. She and Sarah liked to exchange tacky cowgirl presents. The hokier, the better, and the pajamas happened to be the worst of all. They also happened to be the most comfortable item of clothing she owned and she wore them almost every night. Even now as she made her way into the honky-tonk, she wore the top under her black leather jacket.

Her hair was tied on top of her head in a messy bun, and makeup was almost nonexistent. She really hadn't planned on going anywhere but to the kitchen for more food when Milo had insisted she stop brooding and get out for the night. She'd already shed a few thousand tears so she was all cried out at the moment. A few hours at Belly Up, her old haunt, seemed like a great alternative to sadness.

"That cowboy needs a strong dose of some Briggs tough love."

"I don't know if either of us is ready for everyone to know about our baby."

"The truth's gonna come out sooner or later, may as well be sooner. What he needs to do is man up to his responsibility."

"And do what? Marry me?"

"Sounds about right to me."

But before she could respond, he walked away, leaving her alone in the familiar crowd.

She made her way to the bar. Her friend Kendra Myers worked it tonight looking as beautiful as ever with her black raven hair pulled into a long ponytail, and her petite body shoved into a tight pair of jeans and the black logo tee. Kendra couldn't be more than five feet tall, but she was a force to be reckoned with behind that bar. Give her any kind of grief, and you were out the front door before you knew what happened.

"Well, look at you," Kendra yelled as Helen took a seat at the bar. "I heard you were in town."

Kendra put a white napkin down in front of her.

"I'm sure that's not all you heard," Helen said, getting comfortable on the wooden stool.

"You know I don't pay no mind to what folks say, but I gotta admit, this time they were right. How far along are you?"

"Far enough to be uncomfortable every night."

"Sweetie, you need one of those body pillows. You can order it online, or better still you can have one of mine."

"Thanks, but I don't want to—"

"Honey, after five babies I can tell you for a fact, I won't be needing it anymore. Besides, I have two and one of them is brand-new. I'll drop it off tomorrow."

Kendra had started having babies with her high school

sweetheart right after graduation and only stopped two years ago when she turned twenty-five. Ever since she turned twenty-one she worked three nights a week, five hour shifts at the bar to keep her sanity, she said, and without a doubt, Kendra was one of the most sane people Helen knew.

"Thanks, but I'm going back to Jackson in the morning."

"What? But we haven't even had time for a good girl talk. You can't leave yet."

"There's no reason for me to stay." And just as she said it, her eyes watered.

"Oh, honey, what's wrong? You know you can tell me anything."

Helen wiped her eyes with the bar napkin. "It's just that I—"

"Hey, barkeep, we're gettin' dry down here!" a male voice yelled at the other end of the bar.

"Keep your boots on. I'll be right there," she yelled back at him. Then she turned to Helen. "What can I get you?"

"Plain soda, three olives."

Kendra filled the order then walked down to the other end of the bar, warning the customer to cut her some slack or she'd throw him out on his ear. The customer apologized and Kendra poured him and his buddies another round.

Helen took a few sips of her soda then pulled the cocktail pick out of her drink to eat one of the olives when she spotted Colt in the mirror coming up behind her carrying his cream-colored hat in his hands. There was a sheepish grin spread wide across his kissable lips. She turned to face him and they exchanged a smile. The man looked sexier than ever in this lighting. He was dressed in a long-sleeved brown thermal-knit shirt that accentuated his muscular chest and arms, his favorite Wrangler jeans hugged his hips and his polished tan boots spoke volumes. When a cowboy polished his boots for a woman, it usually meant he had courtin' on his mind.

"Treat her good, cowboy," Helen heard Kendra say behind her. "Or you'll have to answer to me."

"I'll do my best," Colt answered.

Helen desperately wished she'd worn something less comfortable, like a dress and heels or anything other than a pajama top. She tried to straighten out the collar in some weak attempt to make it appear less awful. "I wasn't expecting to see you here on a weeknight."

"I went over to Milo's, but when no one was home I remembered you might be here. You look beautiful," he said, making her feel even more uncomfortable.

"Hardly."

"Well, I think you do."

"Thanks," she said, then held up the cocktail stick. "Olive?"

He leaned over and slowly slipped one off the stick with his mouth. Just watching him sent a shiver through her body.

"Can I join you?" he said, nodding toward the empty stool next to her.

"I think you already did," she told him.

Colt gingerly sat himself on the stool, secured his hat on his head, chewed and swallowed the olive, then turned toward Kendra and ordered. "I'll have what she's having."

Kendra served him his drink then left the two of them alone. Helen was dying to ask him all sorts of questions about how he was feeling about her news. She wanted to tell him she understood if he'd had a problem believing her, that the news must have come as a complete shock to him. But most of all, she wanted to let him know how angry she was he'd walked away.

Still, it was his turn to say something, his turn to explain. Instead, the silence between them was palpable. She was hoping he'd apologize or tell her he wanted nothing to do with her or their baby. Either way, he needed to say something or why did he come looking for her, anyway?

After an awkward couple of minutes, while Helen seriously contemplated leaving, he apparently summoned the right amount of courage and said, "I want to apologize for leaving you yesterday. I never should have walked away."

At once all her anger and hurt evaporated. "You had me scared, Colt Granger. I didn't know what to think."

He glanced down for a moment, then up at her. "We have a lot to discuss and a lot to wrap our heads around. I just want you to know that I'll do whatever you want me to do. I'm here for you."

That wasn't exactly the follow-up she'd been hoping for. "You want to clarify that, please?"

"The way I figure it, you know best what you expect from me. You tell me and I'll accommodate."

She blinked at him a couple times then took another sip of her soda, trying to grasp his lame offer. "What about what you want?"

"I just want you to be happy."

"Happy? You want me to be happy?" She folded her arms across her chest. "I had to give up the circuit. I was sick almost every day for five solid months. I can't move back into my own house because I need the money the renters are paying me, therefore I'm living with my parents. I don't know the first thing about babies or raising a child and the whole idea of motherhood scares me to distraction. I've never even held a baby and suddenly I have to decide whether or not to nurse this child or bottle-feed the little munchkin. But my biggest problem is that I don't know my true feelings for my baby's daddy because he's always working or when I do get to spend some time with him, he's busy rescuing his boys, which brings me to yet another problem, your uncontrollable boys. What kind of an influence are they going to be on our baby? It worries me to think that one day my baby may end up inside a claw machine. So no, happiness is not even re-motely a possibility."

She shook from the eruption of emotions she'd been systematically controlling ever since she learned she was pregnant. It felt good to finally let it all out, and even better to lay it on Colt, who seemed almost indifferent to her tirade.

She waited, hoping he'd take her in his arms and tell her everything would be okay, desperately needing the physical contact, craving the warmth of his touch, of his assurance that he'd be there for her no matter what. She needed him to say something and not walk away again.

Instead he just stared at her, his eyes taking in her face. Then he stood, and she wanted to scream right there in the bar. He was leaving again, pulling out some cash for the drinks and getting ready to leave.

She wanted to yell at the top of her lungs. Wanted Kendra to come over and throw him out. Wanted him banned from the bar forever. Wanted him…

"Let's get out of here," he said in a low, sexy voice, reaching out for her hand.

He wore a wicked little grin and she knew their argument was over, at least for the time being, so she took his hand.

TWENTY MINUTES LATER, her cowgirl pajama top was lying on the floor along with the rest of her clothes in Milo's tiny guest bedroom. A night-light illuminated the colorful room from a floor socket next to the double bed. The curtains were open just enough to let in the moon's glow. Helen hated complete darkness when she slept, so much so that she always carried a night-light when she traveled and kept a battery-powered lantern next to her bed in case the electricity went out in the middle of the night.

She watched Colt pull off his boots, and she helped him with his shirt and pants as he gently caressed her breasts then glided his hands over her round belly. Soon they were naked as they stood together, with him moving behind her as he gently caressed her baby bump.

"I never stopped thinking about you since the night we made love."

"Me, neither. I've been so worried about telling you," she told him as her voice hitched and her eyes watered. He turned her around to face him.

"Don't cry, sweetheart. I'm here now."

He softly kissed each of her eyelids and she melted into him as they moved onto the bed and lay side by side, facing each other, getting to know each other's bodies once again. She wrapped a leg around his hip while the other one rested in between his legs. She stroked his muscled chest, his strong back, then glided her fingers across his abdomen. He shivered and she knew this was so right. This was their destiny. They were finally on the right course.

"I tried to tell you about our baby so many times, but something always stopped me."

He ran his hand gently over her swollen breasts. Heat rushed over her body, sending tiny shivers down to her toes. She basked in his touch, slightly arching her back in response. Wanting more of the same. Wanting him to never stop. He kissed her neck, then each of her breasts, until she moaned with pleasure. Then he slowly made his way back up to her mouth, kissing and caressing her as he carefully pulled her in tighter against his body.

"Could that something be my boys?" he whispered.

She nodded and dusted her lips on his, then they sank into a passionate kiss that set her soul on fire. It felt so good to be in his arms again, to have him touch her, caress her, make love to her, that she could hardly control her emotions. When his fingers tempted her further it didn't take much for her to react with a fierce shudder.

"I've missed you," he whispered. "You're all I've been thinking about."

Despite the sincerity in his voice, she wondered if that was true. Wondered if he'd ever thought of her at all. He seemed to be dating every single woman in town. Why would he think of her?

But her negative thoughts vanished when he tenderly guided her under him.

"Me, too," she whispered as she nipped his earlobe and wrapped her legs around his hips, causing him to slow down.

They moved together easily, gently, as if Colt was a little afraid of hurting her, of hurting their baby. The intensity wasn't there like it had been the first time they made love. This was different and she liked it; more sensual, more romantic than the first time.

She tried to increase the rhythm, but each time Colt eased it up again. Finally, she gave in and surrendered to his tempo, and when she did, she found her release to be more blissful than anything she'd ever experienced. She could get used to this kind of lovemaking, this kind of slow burn.

As their breathing evened out and he moved off her, and she spooned up next to him, she couldn't help wondering if he felt the same way.

"Colt, I'm leaving in the morning."

He turned and pushed himself up on the bed, pulling the blankets over them. "No, you're not. We're just getting started."

"I don't know what that means exactly."

"It means, Helen Shaw, will you—"

She stopped him from saying another word. Apprehension tickled her stomach. "I don't think we're ready to get married. It may sound strange, but we don't know enough about each other. Not really. And you have three boys. I'm not sure if I can handle one boy let alone three. I'm just not ready. I don't—"

He looked at her and smiled. "I agree. So that's why I want to ask you. Helen Shaw, will you date me?"

She laughed. "Colt Granger, you are the *darnedest* cowboy."

"Is that a yes?"

"Yes, I'd love to date you."

He grinned and kissed her, but in the middle of the kiss, he pulled back. "You never told me. Is it a boy or a girl?"

"I don't know. I asked the doctor not to tell me. I'm guessing it's a boy, but I'm hoping for a girl."

"When's your next appointment with the doctor?"

"A couple weeks. Why?"

"I'd like to come with you."

He ran a finger down her cheek and along her lips. Heat danced over her skin and she wanted him to make love to her all over again. "Sure, if you can get the time." She grinned.

She moved in closer, ready to be swept away. Ready

for him to prove to her that this thing they had for each other might genuinely grow into something more meaningful.

"Time! *Shoot*. What time is it?"

There was a digital clock on the nightstand behind her and Colt lifted his head to check it out.

"Darlin', I hate to do this." He kissed her. "I mean I really hate to do this." He kissed her again, deeper this time. "But I have to leave. Mrs. Abernathy warned me that I had to be home by ten—no staying out all night—or she would report me to the police that I've abandoned my boys. I believe that woman would do it, too."

Helen glanced at the clock. He had twenty minutes to drive back to the Granger ranch. He would be cutting it close. "You better hurry." And she kissed him, hard.

"You make me want to stay."

She chuckled. "Just giving you a little something extra to keep you warm on the way home."

"Darlin', if I was any warmer, my boys would be calling me from the police station."

"Then you better get your hustle on because you now have less than twenty minutes to drive home."

Colt reluctantly slipped out of bed and was in and out of the bathroom and dressed in less time than it took for Helen to get up and throw on her robe. The room was cold and her body temperature had quickly fallen.

He gave her a brief kiss while standing in the bedroom doorway. "See you tomorrow?"

"I'll be here."

He grinned, gave her another kiss and rushed out of the room.

As she listened to him clomp down the stairs and shut the front door behind him, an intense feeling of uncertainty came over her.

What on earth could have come over her? Sheer terror overtook her when she thought of being responsible for Colt's boys.

She shook it off and forced herself to think of only good thoughts, like their lovemaking, and of taking their relationship one day at a time.

Her mind spun faster with a wedding scenario, and of her round, protruding belly under a white dress and everyone staring at her as she walked down the aisle, shaking their heads, whispering how she'll never be able to corral those boys; of Joey getting ready to jump from the choir box in the chapel, his legs dangling over the guests in the pews. And of Gavin getting stuck in back of the altar. Buddy calling to their father to come help as the local fire department came charging in, axes raised.

She shivered, crawled back into bed and stared up at the white ceiling, totally mortified…and did the only thing she was truly good at anymore.

She sobbed.

Chapter Six

Colt made it home with two minutes to spare. When he walked in the door his boys were still awake and came rushing over to him in a stampede of questions. "Is it true, Papa?" Joey wanted to know. "You have some really great news?"

The enthusiasm caught Colt completely by surprise.

"I don't know what you're talking about, Joey," he said, stalling, wondering what they'd heard and who had done the gossiping.

"Dad, Milo said you have some big news to share. What is it, Dad? What?" Buddy asked as he pulled on Colt's arm.

"We can't stand it, Daddy. We have to know what it is," Gavin demanded as he held on to Colt's belt. "He wouldn't give us any details, just that we had to ask you. So now we're asking you. What's the news?"

"Wait a minute. Did Milo stop by?" He gazed over at Mrs. Abernathy.

"Nope, I took them to the drive-in for an early feature because they needed entertaining and that busybody Milo Gump mentioned something about you and Helen having big news, then one thing led to another and before I knew it, he was telling everybody at the concession stand how you and Helen have a secret to share. That was after those boys of yours ordered up enough burgers and Spud Buds to feed half of Briggs." She motioned for Colt to come a little closer to her. He broke away from his sons, and did as he was told. She whispered in his ear, "Does this have something to do with Helen's baby?"

He really didn't want to admit it so soon, but now that Milo was telling people at the concession stand, the whole town would know by morning.

"I have to admit that it does."

"Are you the daddy?"

It was times like these that he wished he lived in New York City. "Yes, ma'am, I am."

"Uh-huh. I assume you two will be getting hitched-up soon."

"What? No. We're dating, is all."

She shrugged. "Appears to be a little late in the game for dating, but you young folks all seem to do things backward these days."

"Neither one of us wants to rush into anything."

"The horse is already out of the barn on that one, Colt, and halfway out of town, for that matter." She then went over to the sofa and gathered her things.

Colt didn't care much for her response, but then Mrs. Edith Abernathy was a woman who spoke her mind, no matter what the outcome. And truth be told, he always liked that about her.

What really bothered him was the fact that Milo had taken it upon himself to tell his boys, and apparently anybody else who would listen, about his affair with Helen. Okay, so maybe he hadn't come right out with every detail, but with Helen's prominent baby bump and no daddy around, it wouldn't take much for everyone in Briggs to figure things out.

Still, Milo could've waited for a couple days so he could break the news to his boys on his own terms. Now he had no choice but to come clean.

"I'll be going home now, and I won't be coming back anytime soon," Mrs. Abernathy said. "I've got me some important planning to do and it's going to take all my time."

"What kind of planning?" Buddy asked as he and his brothers once again jumped on Colt. This time they nearly knocked him down with their enthusiasm.

"You'll have to talk to your grandpa Dodge about that one."

She slipped on her tweed wool coat, wrapped a green scarf around her weathered neck and turned to the boys. "Now you boys listen up." Her voice took on a commanding sound, as if she was about to tell the troops what the battle plan would be.

They stopped pulling on Colt and stood at attention in a shoulder to shoulder lineup—Buddy, then Gavin, then Joey. Colt loved the power this woman had over his sons. He didn't know what she did to get them to behave, but whatever it was, he was all for it.

"You mind your daddy, ya hear? He don't need you getting in no more trouble. Gavin, you stay out of them machines."

"Yes, ma'am."

"And, Joey, you stay off of that there roof on your grandpa's property. You about gave everybody a heart attack."

Joey straightened up before he answered, "Yes, ma'am."

"And, Buddy, I expect you to start curbing your brothers' bad behavior. You're the oldest, and you got a responsibility to your dad to help out. Do you understand me?"

"Yes, ma'am."

"Now y'all come on over here and give me some lovin'."

All three boys followed her orders with hugs and kisses. It was truly a precious sight for Colt to witness. They were as gentle with her as pups to their mama. It made him reconsider his boys' foolish ways. Maybe he stood a chance of raising fine, upstanding citizens after all. With Mrs. Abernathy's help, of course.

Colt walked over to the door. "Let me see you out."

"Thanks," she told him as she slipped on her fur-lined leather gloves. Then she and Colt strolled out into the brisk night air. Mrs. Abernathy tightened her scarf around her neck.

"It sure is cold early this year," she said.

"Means we have a good chance at an early spring," Colt answered.

Once Mrs. Abernathy was in her fire-red SUV, with the engine started, she powered down her window and said, "You got yourself a good woman in Helen. She's a little high-spirited like them boys of yours, but she'll be a good mother to your baby. And don't be scared. She's going to be all right. When the time comes, I'll be at her side. You can count on it."

Mrs. Abernathy was still a practicing RN and had helped half the women in Briggs deliver their babies. She acted as a support person for both the mom and the dad. She knew exactly when it was time to go to the hospital, and once there, she'd stay with the parents to help in any way she could. She'd been there for all three of Colt's boys, and he hoped she could be there for this baby, as well.

"That would mean a lot to me. Thanks."

"And about you and Helen dating and not wanting to rush into anything, don't you know anything about women yet? It ain't what you say. It's what you do."

"It's been a while since I went courting a woman."

"Nothing's changed. It might seem like it has with all them electronic gadgets, but in the end you two gotta know for certain what you feel in your heart. Nothing else matters."

"I'll try to work on that. You're a smart woman, Edith, and we're lucky to have you in our lives."

She reached out and patted his hand. "You sure are, and so is Dodge. He's the luckiest dude in the valley."

She chuckled and drove off into the night as Colt's boys anxiously waited on the front porch for him to tell them the big news.

"She can't be our mother. She's nothing like our mother. Our mother's dead!" Buddy insisted as Colt tried his best to make his boys understand the situation. So far he was failing miserably. The boys had jumped to the conclusion that if Helen was the mother to their new little brother or sister, then she would be their mother, as well. Colt had tried to explain that wasn't the case, but they couldn't seem to understand the difference.

Colt and his boys were sitting at the kitchen table drinking hot chocolate, and dressed in their pajamas. They were up late for a school night but Colt felt this was important enough to settle before he put them to bed. He thought they'd be as pleased as all get out that they were going to have another sibling. Instead they were about as happy as finding a rattler in their beds.

"I'd have to marry Helen in order for her to be your new mom."

"Are you going to marry her?" Buddy asked, looking sullen.

"I don't know that yet."

"Does that mean you *might* marry her?"

Buddy was always too smart for his years. "I'm not ruling it out."

"Would we have to call her mom?" Gavin asked.

"You boys are getting way ahead of things here. All I'm trying to tell you is that Helen's baby will be part of our family, regardless if we get married or not."

"Don't you want to marry Helen, Papa?" Joey asked with a hot cocoa mustache.

Colt let out a sigh. "We need to get to know each other first."

"But you already know each other, Papa. That doesn't make sense."

"We need to know each other better."

"I don't want you to marry Helen. We already have a mom," Buddy insisted, plunking his mug down on the table, causing some of the liquid to spill out. "Sorry," he said and wiped up the mess with his napkin.

"And nobody will ever take your mom's place in your heart."

Colt never expected his boys would react so negatively to the prospect of his getting remarried. He always assumed they would welcome another woman into their lives.

"If she was our mother, would we have to mind her?" Joey asked.

"Yes, you'd have to mind her just like you have to mind me."

"That's no fun," Joey declared. Colt handed him a napkin and motioned for him to wipe his mouth. He did, then he placed it on his lap the way Colt had taught him.

"She's fun now because she lets us do whatever we want to do," Gavin explained. "If she's our mother she won't let us do anything. Everything will change. We don't need another mother and we don't want another brother or sister...."

"Don't you love our mom anymore?" Buddy asked, his expression bordering on tears.

"Of course I do, and I always will. But that doesn't mean I can't love another woman, as well."

"Are you gonna have two wives, Papa?" Joey wanted to know.

"What? No. I won't have two wives and you won't have two moms."

"Oh, yes, we will," Gavin said. "You ruined everything!"

And he stormed off to his room.

"We're only dating," Colt yelled after him. "It's not like we're even considering getting married."

But Gavin had already slammed his door shut. Colt had never seen him so angry.

He turned to Buddy, who had gotten very quiet. "I thought you would be the happiest, son. Helen's an expert rider. Once the baby's born she'll be able to pick up where I left off. You said you wanted to learn how to jump. Helen can teach you how to do that."

"She's not a jumper. She's a shooter. She doesn't know anything about equestrian stuff. That's a different sport. And besides, once that little baby gets here she won't want to do anything with us."

"That's not true, son. She'll want to do lots of things with you and your brothers."

"We get into too much trouble," Joey said. "Nobody wants to do anything with us."

Colt countered, "You boys are spirited, is all."

"Joey's right," Buddy said, sliding off his chair. "*You* don't even want to do stuff with us anymore, why should Helen?"

A twinge of guilt gripped Colt's stomach. He'd been working so hard on the ranch, fixing tractors, mending fences, checking on the livestock with Travis every day, vaccinating, caring for their ailments, hauling feed and dealing with all aspects of the harvest that he'd been putting things off with his boys. "I'm sorry if you feel that way, son, I…"

But Buddy had already stomped off, slamming the same bedroom door. He shared the room with Gavin. Normally, Colt would never tolerate such behavior, but he figured he'd give them a pass when it came to their emotions about their mother. Losing her had been, in some ways, harder on them than it had been on Colt. Especially on Buddy, who had followed her around like a puppy dog.

Colt turned to Joey in a last-ditch effort to make him understand that his marriage, if it ever happened, and that was a big whopper of an "if," would be a good thing.

"What do you think, son?"

Joey swung his feet back and forth under the table. "Will she have to move in here with us?"

"I reckon so, yes."

"Where will she sleep?"

"With me."

"Does that mean we won't be able to sleep with you when we're scared?"

"Not every time, but we can make exceptions."

Joey thought about that for a moment then took a couple good long gulps of his hot chocolate. When he was finished, he wiped his mouth on his napkin, folded it and placed it next to his cup. He stared over at Colt. "Where will her baby sleep?"

"Probably with us for a while, then in its own room. You'll have to bunk in with your brothers."

"How come the baby gets to sleep with you and Helen and we don't?"

"Because you boys have your own rooms."

"But you just said the baby will have its own room. Why can't you put it in there right away?"

"Because newborn babies need to be close to their mothers."

"Did I sleep with my mother?"

"You slept with me, son."

"Where was my mother, Papa?"

"In heaven with God."

"Didn't she like me, Papa?" Big tears tumbled out of his eyes and slid down his chubby little cheeks. For the first time in a long time, Colt realized how small and vulnerable Joey was.

The question broke Colt's heart. Joey hadn't ever really questioned him about his mother. Colt had always known the subject would come up one day and he'd prepared countless speeches for it, but never had he prepared for this.

"Come on over here, son," Colt urged, patting his lap for his boy to come and sit. Joey climbed up and laid his head on his father's chest. Colt stroked his blond hair thinking how it felt like silk and how his late wife, Karen, would have pampered and loved this boy. He looked just like her and sometimes, when he was sleeping, he knew she was lying right there with him, singing him a lullaby.

"Your mama couldn't wait for you to be born. You made her happy each and every day. I remember one day in particular when she was watching me hang the cowboy wallpaper you still have in your room, when she finally decided on your name, Joseph Dodge Granger. After that, she always referred to you as her little Joey."

"It was her papa's name, right?"

"Yep, plus my papa's name."

"Is my other grandpa up in heaven with Mama?"

"I suspect they're both in heaven watching over you and your brothers."

"Do you think Mama likes Helen?"

"I think she does because Helen is good to her little Joey, and Buddy and Gavin and me. And your mama knows that Helen is a very special lady who will need all the respect and kindness we can give her."

Joey yawned and rubbed his eyes with his fists just like he did when he was a baby. Colt picked him up, carried him to his room, tucked him in bed and gave him his favorite stuffed animal. Joey still slept with his now tattered brown bunny. The bunny his mother bought him a week before he was born.

"Papa, I hope Helen moves in with us."

Colt kissed his son's forehead, happy that at least one of his boys had finally accepted her. He knelt down on one knee next to the bed, and brushed Joey's curls out of his eyes.

"Why's that, son?"

"She makes better hot cocoa than you do."

HELEN SPENT THE next week in Jackson with her parents. Milo's house was fine, but Helen had too many things she needed to do to justify hanging around his place. She knew Tater was in good hands with Milo, so she drove home the next afternoon.

Even though she and Colt couldn't see each other like

they had hoped to, they spent every night on the phone in long conversations about each other's day. Helen found herself looking forward to hearing his reassuring voice after a busy day of shopping and appointments as she waded through her new life. Lately, each and every day was consumed by baby preparations. Between learning how to create healthy organic food, courtesy of her eager female cousins, going to doctor's appointments, remembering to take an assortment of vitamins at different times of the day, which her stepmom had sorted out for her in little plastic containers, to getting the right amount of exercise, to deciding on the type of birthing classes she wanted to take, her main focus had gone from winning a championship to everything maternal.

"I can't seem to relax," she told Kendra as she parked her monster SUV in front of the baby supplies store that Kendra had insisted on driving her to even though it was about an hour away from both Jackson and Briggs. It was the mega baby store that Kendra had shopped at for all her babies, and according to Kendra, no other store could touch it.

Helen's stepmom wanted to join them, but at the last minute she decided to stay in bed and nurse a cold she'd been fighting for the past couple of days. Helen considered driving to the store on her own, but she didn't know the first thing about what she needed for this baby let alone what she should register for. Kendra and Helen's stepmom, Janet, were throwing her a baby shower in the next couple of weeks, so Helen needed to start picking out what she wanted…as if making those decisions was even remotely possible.

"Just go with the flow, sweetie, and you'll be fine," Kendra told Helen as they walked through the open automatic doors.

"Wow!" Helen couldn't believe her eyes. The store was massive. Baby stuff for as far as the eye could see, and then some. "Shouldn't Colt be here? After all, he's done all this three times before. Surely he'd know exactly what the baby needs."

Whereas this was totally foreign to Helen. It felt as if she was walking into an alien world and someone said, *Now go and thrive.*

"Did somebody say my name?" Colt said as he came out from behind a counter filled with baby bottles and sterilizers.

At once Helen felt relieved and walked right up to him and gave him a tight hug, grateful that he'd taken the time to be there for her. He felt safe and strong, and all she wanted to do was stand there and kiss him.

"Thanks for this, Colt," she whispered in his ear. "I can't do this on my own."

"I wouldn't want you to, darlin'."

And he kissed her, a brush of a kiss, but enough for the memory of their lovemaking to spark through her body, causing her to slightly flush.

Somehow he'd gotten more good-looking since the other night, if that was even possible, or she was falling hard for this cowboy and seeing him through emotion rather than reality. Either way, the view was spectacular.

"That's why we're here," Kendra said with a lilt to her voice. "They carry organic cotton baby clothes, and untreated wooden cribs. You wouldn't want to put your baby in anything synthetic. I didn't know any better with my first baby and made some terrible mistakes. Poor thing was allergic to almost everything. It wasn't until I read about organics and I made the switch when my second baby was born that my son got over his allergies. Anything that's not earth friendly shouldn't be in the same room as a newborn. I think they even carry organic cotton crib sheets and receiving blankets. You can never have too many receiving blankets."

Helen could see the sparkle in Kendra's eyes as she looked around at pink make-your-own-baby-food blenders, and something she kept calling a receiving blanket—obviously a big deal to her—and extremely scary-looking breast pumps.

"Relax," Colt told Helen, privately while Kendra was out of earshot. "Kendra's just excited about helping you. After three boys, I can tell you for a fact, organic or synthetic, that little baby won't care a hoot as long as you're holding it in your arms."

Helen leaned into him and he kissed her again. She could get used to his kisses, his soothing voice and his cowboy ways. Too bad he represented everything she'd worked so hard to avoid.

A friendly young woman with long blond hair and dazzling white teeth sat behind a desk and filled in a form on a computer screen with the answers Helen gave her. She wanted Helen's due date, her full name, address, phone number and the sex of the baby. Helen told her she thought it was a boy, but the woman typed in *TBD* because technically Helen wasn't sure yet. When the girl completed the form she handed Helen an electronic pad, and told her to just scan everything and anything she wanted. "The pad is all set up for you. It will pick up the scans, sort them out and create a registry for you. It's simple. You can always add or delete things online once you get home."

Helen nodded her agreement, feeling as if she was in some sort of baby-buying fog.

Kendra led the way and Helen and Colt followed. As Kendra pointed out bottles, strollers, changing tables, cribs and non-BPA breast pumps, an important assumption arose. "Of course you'll be breast-feeding and the best pump is this one." She pointed to a type of pump that apparently sucked out a woman's milk from both breasts at once.

"I'd feel like a cow using that thing," Helen said. She hadn't even seriously considered whether or not she would breast-feed her baby. The thought of a baby suckling on her breast scared her, and made her a little nauseous at the same time.

"I never really used it for my own babies. They were only breast-fed, but I would donate milk to the hospital for premature babies or to help out moms who couldn't breast-feed. I'm not saying that you should do either of those things, sweetie, but in case you want to, this pump extracts your milk at the same rate that your baby would. Your nipples won't even get sore. But in case they do, there's a wonderful cream I can recommend."

"Maybe *you* should carry this pad thing around. You seem to know exactly what I need."

Helen handed her the electronic pad and Kendra took off up the aisle, scanning all sorts of things on the way. Helen was sure when she finally had the baby shower and she received all the gifts, Kendra would have to come over to instruct her on usage.

"Don't mind her. After five babies, I expect she's thrilled to be talking to a brand-new mom," Colt said, half chuckling.

"I have to admit, I'm overwhelmed with all of this. And Kendra. I had no idea she would get so excited about a baby. She's nothing like this behind a bar."

"It's a lot for you to take in at one time."

"More than you know."

Kendra waved them over to the crib section of the store, just as Helen began to feel a bit woozy.

"We won't be needing a new crib, even though Kendra will probably try to persuade you to get one. Got a real nice one stored out in the barn. We bought it new for Joey."

Helen nodded as she envisioned an entire barn filled with cribs, blankets, blenders, sterilizers, bottles and a multitude of brightly colored toys—with walls painted sky-blue, and no animals in the barn, just a monster breast pump set up in the center waiting for her to sit down and attach her breasts to it. Panic began to take hold. Her chest tightened and she couldn't breathe. Sweat beaded on her forehead.

"You don't look so good. Are you all right?" Colt asked.

He suddenly looked panicked, which caused Helen to panic and want to get out of there. She wanted to get away from Colt, away from everything baby. "I don't feel good. I can't...breathe. I need fresh air."

And she headed for the front door, with Colt trailing up behind her.

"You had a panic attack," Doctor Bradley Starr said as Helen sat on the sofa in Colt's living room. Gavin and Buddy were still in school and Joey was with his grandfather. Kendra had just left to pick up her youngest from day care. "You need to rest."

"I've never had a panic attack in my entire life. Not ever," Helen told him, rubbing her upper chest. It still hurt from the spasm she'd had in the store.

"There's always a first time for everything."

She had wanted Kendra to drive her back home, but Colt thought it best if she drive over to his house. It was closer. Helen was in no condition to argue, so she went along with the program. As soon as they were in the car, Colt phoned the doctor to meet them. He'd assured her that it was easier than taking her to a hospital, especially since she wasn't having any issues with the baby.

Doctor Starr was a general practitioner who did house calls and was used to treating Colt and his boys. Plus, he worked in the same office as Helen's doctor two days a week in Jackson, which made him familiar with Helen's pregnancy. It seemed easy for the doctor to diagnose her. All he had to do was look at her and he knew exactly what was going on. "Panic attacks are quite common during a pregnancy, especially with your first."

"My only," Helen stated without reservation. No way did she want any more children. One was quite enough.

"Then you'll have to learn what triggers these episodes and take the proper precautions. Realistically, you might very well have another panic attack before the baby's due date."

"I was merely shopping for baby things."

"Where?"

"That huge store, the one off the highway."

"That place would give *me* a panic attack. I bet that was Kendra's idea."

"How'd you guess?"

"With five children, Kendra's a well-seasoned mother. You're a rookie. She should've known better and started you off slowly, maybe with a pair of booties."

Helen thought of tiny baby booties, blue baby booties, or pink. She hadn't really thought of pink before. What if it was a girl? Her chest tightened as Colt walked into the room carrying a tray with everything she needed for a cup of hot tea. Nope, just seeing all that rugged testosterone walk toward her convinced her there was no way that man could produce anything but boys.

The thought seemed to calm her. She understood boys, or at least she knew how to relate to them better than little girls.

Colt brought in three mugs, sugar, milk and a large white teapot filled with hot water. He'd also brought an assortment of tea bags, and cookies, as if he'd been serving up high tea his entire life. Who knew?

"Can I get you anything else?" Colt asked, looking a little more like his old self. A more normal color had returned to his face. At one point during the drive, Helen was more worried for Colt than for herself.

"Thanks, that's perfect," Helen told him just as he rubbed her shoulder, then took a seat next to her on the sofa.

The doctor filled in the details about Helen's panic attack, took her temperature, listened to her heart, then demonstrated a breathing technique to help her ward off another one. After he drank down his tea, packed up his black bag and said his goodbyes, the doctor walked out to his car and headed back to town, leaving Helen and Colt alone.

"I'm scared, Colt," Helen told him while reclining on the sofa. Her baby moving inside her only increased her fears. "My stepmom is great, and I really love her, but I really wish my mom was still alive. We never got to talk about babies, or being pregnant, or what it took to raise a child. She died when I was only fourteen. Too young for us to have that conversation. And even if she'd lived through my teens, a baby was the last thing on my mind. Learning how to shoot and ride was all I cared about. A competitive time in the event meant everything to me. And now? Here I sit, ready to bring a child into the world and I don't have any idea of how to mother a child or what to do with all those things I saw in that store today. Ask me about horses and riding and shooting and I can fill a book. Ask me about mixing a drink and I can write another book from all my years working in bars. But babies? I couldn't fill a page on a clipboard let alone one chapter of a book. I never really considered nursing my baby or whether or not I should puree its first food or buy it in a jar. And don't even get me started on wooden verses plastic cribs, organic baby clothes or synthetic. And why on earth does someone need so many receiving blankets? And why are they called receiving blankets? They look like regular baby blankets to me. I don't even know what half of those things mean. I'm scared, Colt. Scared I won't be able to do it right." She sighed as big hot tears slipped down her cheeks.

He knelt down next to her on the floor, pulled out his hankie and handed it to her, then lovingly stroked her face and head.

She wiped her eyes and sniffled into the hankie, grateful that once again he was prepared for her waterworks.

"I think you're going to make a wonderful mother," he told her in a deep, reassuring voice. "All you need to know are the basics, and that will come automatically the first time you hold your baby. You're going to be fine, I promise. Besides, there is no right way to do this, there's only your way, and if it's filled with the kind of love I know you have for this child, everything will fall into place. I'm sure of it."

His fingers traced her cheek, and she moved in closer to him.

"I want to believe you, but my head won't stop spinning. A shower? A registry? Do we really need all of that stuff? Wouldn't it be easier if we bought what we needed for the baby at Diamond's in town?" Diamond's was the town's one and only department store, which fit entirely on one floor.

"It's what folks do when they're having a baby."

"That doesn't make it necessary."

"No, but it's supposed to be fun. Most women like all this fuss."

"I'm not the average woman. I'd rather be shooting from the saddle of a horse."

"Then we won't do it. We'll order what you want for the baby online. How's that?"

Helen thought about it for a moment then she sat up and shook her head.

"I can't do that. My friends will be disappointed. And my stepmom will be upset as well, then my dad will be angry at me for upsetting his wife. It's a no-win situation."

"I didn't know this was a race."

She sighed again. "It's not. But I can't just let go like that."

Colt sat next to her, slid down a little on the sofa, and she rested her head on his chest.

She said, "It's hard for me, Colt. I overreacted today, overthought everything. How can I let a little thing like a baby get me so upset?"

"Hormones?"

"Maybe that's it. Maybe I need to learn to relax more. Meditate. Do yoga."

He took her hand in his. "Let me take care of you. I know you like to be in charge of every aspect of your life, but things are different now. I want to be a part of our baby's life. I'm here for whatever you need."

She felt uneasy at the thought of depending on another person, even if it was the father of her child. "That's hard for me. I've always taken care of myself. Known what I wanted and gone out and made it happen. I haven't had someone take care of me or counsel me since I was ten, and even then I had already made up my mind about my future."

"You're in a different phase of your life now, sweetheart. It's time you allowed other people to help you. That way, you won't be so stressed and you won't give me any more scares."

She sat up and looked at him. She knew better than to rile him during her pregnancy, knew he would be overly concerned about every little event. This was not the time for her to fall apart. If anything, she needed to be the strong one, needed to take the bull by the horns, so to speak.

"It'll take me a while to learn how to let go."

"That's fine, but at least you'll be walking on the right road."

The whole idea of letting go of the decisions that concerned her life was like letting go of her ability to breathe on her own. Her life had been spent learning how to stand on her own two feet and just when she'd gotten closer than ever before, it felt as if it was slipping away from her. She couldn't concede and still be true to herself. It had been difficult enough for her to allow her parents and cousins to dote on her while she was busy thinking of what to do next, but now Colt wanted in on the game.

"I'll try, but I'll do it my way."

"And how's that?"

"I need to learn more about all this baby stuff so I

can make informed decisions. Where do you keep your laptop? I want to read up on a suitable breast pump. I've decided I'm nursing my baby."

Chapter Seven

Helen found that she simply couldn't ride as easily as she once could. Just like the doctor in Vegas had predicted, her balance had become a bit shaky. She didn't want to admit she was so fragile that she couldn't ride and could barely maintain Tater on her own. It was like admitting she'd failed at something, and Helen prided herself on never giving up or giving in.

Unfortunately, like Dr. Starr had said, there was always a first time for everything.

She had ventured back to the mega baby store several times on her own without having a panic attack. Now she could walk through the store with little more than a hiccup and a snort. She decided against a formal baby shower, much to Kendra's dismay. Instead, she'd made her first purchase, an infant car seat that snapped onto a stroller base in case she ever wanted to take her baby into town for a little stroll with its daddy, Colt. The man who had just pulled his horse trailer up to the front of Milo's stable.

It was a bigger horse trailer than she'd expected Colt to bring, one that held two horses. The same one he'd used when she first bought Tater from him. He'd even hitched it to his old pickup instead of his SUV.

Part of her couldn't believe she was doing this, and Milo was right there to tell her it was a mistake.

"You're going to miss not having Tater out in my stable to ride whenever you have a hankering to," he told her as he leaned against the doorjamb to the stable. His tan felt hat sat high on his head, and his forehead creased with worry lines. "Just like you could ride him at will when he was boarded with the Miltons. Now you'll have to call first to make an appointment to ride him at the Grangers'."

"No, I won't," Helen countered. "You're just saying that to keep him here. I can't do that. Not for the winter. I won't be driving in from Jackson much with a baby. At least if he's boarded at the Grangers' stable he won't be alone. Colt will ride him a lot more than I can."

It had been a hard decision to make, considering she would now be dependent on Colt for something else— the well-being of her horse. She had to force herself to let go, to allow Colt to help her, and she knew there was no better way for him to help than to board Tater. Besides, she knew Tater would be a lot happier in a large stable with other horses.

Milo's stable was once crowded with no less than six horses at any one time, but going on three years ago, when one of his stallions accidentally stepped on the back of his foot and put Milo out of commission for six months, he'd sold all his horses. His stable had been empty ever since except for Tater, who seemed sad all by himself in that great span of empty space.

Besides, Colt had been worried about her being around Tater, and had no problem voicing his opinion. He felt certain Tater would someday kick her or throw her, neither of which Tater had ever done or would ever do. He was the sweetest, most agreeable horse she'd ever had the privilege of working with. She'd been around horses since she was three years old and had never had any kind of an injury. Despite Colt having grown up around horses, and all the stories she'd heard of his mom riding into town to buy groceries while she was pregnant with her boys, that wasn't enough to persuade him into thinking that nothing bad would happen to her if she rode and tended to Tater.

When it was all said and done, it was simply easier on their budding relationship if she let Tater go for a while. Then, once the baby was a few months old, there'd be no stopping her. At least that was the promise she made to herself.

Colt secured the back ramp for Tater, and the sound of that ramp hitting the ground, combined with what Milo had said, caused Helen's conviction to falter for a moment. Was she doing the right thing? Was this something she wanted to do or was this what Colt wanted?

She sighed, knowing either way, this was a done deal.

She walked past Milo into the stable and up to Tater's stall. He always knew when something was up and today was no exception. He stood stock-still in the back of the stall when he usually came walking right up to the front to greet her whenever she came near. He'd bob his head over the door, eager for an apple or a pat. This time he merely whinnied but didn't move.

"Come on, boy. I promise to come visit you every chance I get."

He blew out some air, bobbed his fine head and stomped his right front leg, but he still wouldn't move from the back of the stall.

She opened the stall door and he gingerly took a couple steps toward her then stopped again, his dark, honey-colored mane flopping between his eyes. She'd brushed him longer than usual that morning, and his creamy dappled coat gave off a healthy glow when the sunlight hit it through the window. He looked stunning standing regally in front of her. He was truly a magnificent creature.

Colt had rescued him from the planes of North Dakota after a roundup less than three years ago, so Tater had a fondness for Colt that was unshakable. He was a wild horse that had claimed her heart from the first moment she met him. She'd trained him herself, and he'd turned out to be the best animal she'd ever known.

Her emotions got the best of her when she thought of the very first time she rode him and tears clouded her eyes. She'd already haltered him with a lead rope that she'd tied in a cowboy knot around his neck so she didn't have to do anything but lead him out when Colt arrived. She thought it would save time and stress.

Apparently Tater had other plans.

Finally, after a little more coaxing, Tater came forward, nudging her with his muzzle. Tears flowed freely as she gave her friend a knowing pat.

Then she pulled herself together, grabbed his lead, moved it over his head while she stood on his left side, like she'd done a million times before, and led him out of the stable.

"I can take him from here," Colt said as she approached.

She shook her head. "Thanks, but I'll trailer him."

"Helen, why can't you let me do this? You know I get worried every time you're around him."

"I've done this a million times, Colt. Tater's not going to hurt me."

"If anything were to happen…"

She touched Colt's arm and could feel his tension. "Relax, I've got this."

Colt let out a frustrated sigh as she hesitated behind the trailer making sure everything on the inside was in perfect order. Before she walked Tater up the ramp, she checked that all the windows were open, there was nothing loose or protruding from the walls, that Milo had dropped some of Tater's favorite hay where he could get at it, which he had, and that the wooden floor looked good and solid.

"It's brand-new," Colt told her, looking all proud of his rig. "Had it installed just last week. Only the best for Tater. That's a promise."

"Thanks," she told him and led Tater in on the left side behind the driver, his hooves clacking on the wood. Colt secured the butt strap and closed the back door while she gave Tater a kiss and left through the open forward escape door, securing it behind her after she exited.

She had planned on going with Colt to make sure Tater liked his new home, but when it came time for her to jump into the passenger seat, she couldn't do it.

"Is it okay if I come over later?" she asked while looking at Colt sitting behind the wheel. "I'll meet you at Pauline's Pumpkin Patch. Will that be all right?"

"Sure. I'll get him settled in. You take your time. I'll take the boys on over around four-thirty. They take a long time to pick out their pumpkins," he told her, looking sympathetic. "And don't be worrying none about Tater. He's going to love it on our ranch. It'll be just like going home for him."

"I know," she said as Milo came up beside her.

"Take good care of that there horse," Milo warned with a gruff voice as if Colt had better abide by his warning.

Colt nodded, turned the engine over and drove off the property with a plume of dust billowing up behind him.

Helen's already queasy stomach tightened, her baby moved and she touched the spot on her large tummy, mentally telling her child how much she loved him... or her.

When Colt was gone from view, Milo turned to her, saying, "Now, you listen up, Helen Shaw." She turned to face him, worried that he was going to lay into her for something or tell her once again how he could take care of Tater just fine.

"Be gentle," she warned him. "I'm fragile and could easily break."

"Not possible. You're solid. Always have been. Always will be."

"I'll try and remember that when my hormones tell me I'm mush."

"Hormones or not, this is what's gonna happen. Are you ready?"

She took a deep breath, stood tall and waited for his best shot, fearing the ultimatum she was sure was coming. "Go for it."

"You're gonna open up that there riding school now instead of waiting until you retire, and I'm gonna help. I've been needin' something to dig my teeth into, and reopening the Miltons' school seems like just the thing for both of us. I don't wanna hear no sass. Just give me some numbers on how much it's gonna cost to get that M & M school up and running 'cause I'm ready to do some business and I'm not taking no for an answer. Do we have ourselves a deal?"

He stuck out his hand.

She gazed at her hulk of a cousin with the heart as big as the universe who always seemed to know exactly what she needed at any given moment and she grinned. Her sweet baby moved again as if spurring her on.

She paused to consider what Colt would think about this idea. Would he find a reason to counsel her against it, or better still she wondered if he'd like to be a part of it, help her run it?

Then reason returned and she knew without a doubt that the Granger ranch was in his blood, part of his DNA, and anything that might dilute that connection had no place in his life.

Helen had to think of her baby now, of making enough money to take care of herself and her child without having to depend on anyone.

Not even Colt.

Without any further hesitation she took Milo's hefty hand in hers. "Cousin, we've got ourselves a deal."

PAULINE'S PUMPKIN PATCH took up several acres of land about a mile north of town. It was the best and only place to find your perfect holiday pumpkin if you lived anywhere in the Teton Valley. Colt took in a deep breath as he sauntered through the colorful leaves that rolled along the ground. There were pumpkins everywhere—on top of stacks of hay, inside wheelbarrows, on tables and stacked on the ground. The air was crisp, the sun hung low in the sky and the trees had a sort of burnt orange glow that reflected off the surrounding barns and stables. What he liked best about Pauline's Pumpkin Patch was that her family also harvested their own apple orchard and made the best cider around, which was served piping hot to everyone who stopped by. The whole experience of Pauline's was one of those traditions that Colt enjoyed sharing with his family, which he hoped would include Helen and their baby in the coming years.

Colt loved this time of year. The crop was in, and it had been a good, profitable one, assuring that the ranch would thrive for yet another year thanks to all their hard work. The livestock was calving with few issues, and so far both mothers and calves seemed healthy, which meant Dodge would have a good showing to sell come next fall. Colt expected a loss during the harsh winter months, but with Travis running the show, and their capable ranch hands looking out for the animals, Colt felt certain most all the calves would survive.

Plus, after giving the consortium all the specifications and details on all the parcels of land he'd looked at, they'd decided to put an offer on the M & M Riding School for the new storage facility. Colt had to admit, he was feeling a little guilty about it after learning Helen's feelings on that piece of property, but it was the best place to build the storage facility. He had to think about the practicality of the business deal and not Helen's emotional ties to the place.

The family lawyer had drawn up the necessary paperwork and everyone had signed it. All that was left to do was to present it to the Miltons, which he would do in the next few days. The way Colt had it figured, next year at this time, the facility would be up and running, and he could rest easy.

Everyone in the Granger family was now hunting for their perfect pumpkin, even Helen. Then later that night, they'd carve their picks at the main house on the Granger ranch. The kids always loved it, but Colt knew the truth of the matter.

The adults loved it even more.

They held a contest, and the best kid's pumpkin carving would get their pumpkin displayed in a prime location on the ranch house porch. The best adult's pumpkin would be showcased in the front window. Dodge had started the tradition when Colt and his brothers were no more than ankle high to a June bug and this years' competition would be no exception.

But at the moment, Colt had a difficult time caring about anything as long as he held Helen in his arms.

"How about if you and me sneak off for about an hour?" Colt whispered in Helen's ear.

His boys had run off to scope out their pumpkins, leaving him and Helen alone for a moment standing in the middle of a field of hundreds of bright orange pumpkins. The blue ribbon winner of the largest pumpkin in the county sat in the back of Pauline's sixty-year-old pink pickup truck parked directly in front of them. This year Pauline's winning pumpkin had weighed in at just over five hundred pounds and drew in fans from as far away as Cody, Wyoming, just to see it.

He pulled her in close. The scent of her ruby hair mingled with the clean scent of the fall air and more than anything Colt wanted to load her up in his SUV, drive home and make love to her slow and easy, all night long.

He was falling hard for this woman who knew exactly how to comfort Joey when he was sick, who could keep up with his boys at a piglet race, who didn't get riled when Gavin was caught in a claw machine, who refused to give up on her dreams and who could make the best hot cocoa this side of the Rockies. Falling for the way she cried for just about anything, and falling for the way she gave herself to him in bed, as if he was the only man in the world she wanted to be with.

She gave him a sly little grin. "You're bad. We can't leave. What about your boys, and your dad and Granger tradition? Aren't we supposed to be picking out pumpkins?"

"Let's you and me start our own tradition. Besides,

I think Dodge is too caught up in Edith to care about traditions."

They glanced over at Dodge as he poured hot cider in a paper cup for Edith, completely smitten by the woman, hardly paying attention to anyone or anything else.

"What do you say, babe? My place is only a few minutes from here."

It was the first time he'd called her *babe*. It felt good. He felt good, good about her, their baby, his boys and life in general. Maybe it was because she'd trusted him with Tater and he felt as though some barrier between them had lifted. That she could depend on him to help her and he'd be there for her. He knew that was a big step for Helen, who prided herself on her independence.

"Colt, I've got something I want to run past you first."

"No need to run past me, darling, I'm standing right here."

A luscious warm smile creased her lips. "This is important, Colt. I want to tell you what I've decided to do. It's something I think will benefit both of us, and your boys, and our baby."

"Can it wait until later?" He brushed her lips with a kiss. She tasted sweet and he wanted more, but she pulled back and he let go of his hold on her.

"Are you this persistent with all your other girlfriends?"

"There are no other girlfriends, only you."

"What about Lana, and Jenny Pickens?"

He looked into her eyes. "You can't be serious? You know those women don't mean anything to me. They were dates my brothers worked up for me. Nothing more. I only want to be with you. You're the only one I care about."

She moved away from him, but kept holding his hand. "You sound serious."

"I am."

She shifted from one leg to the other as he waited for her to tell him she was serious, as well. That she was ready to take their relationship to the next level. He leaned in closer so he could easily kiss her when she told him how much she cared about him.

He waited to hear the words.

Closed his eyes in anticipation.

Then she said, "Colt, I've got to find the ladies' room."

And she ran off to Pauline's Inn, a soft yellow, two-story Victorian nestled in the midst of the pumpkin patch. He watched as she made her way up the front steps. She wore a long blue dress that hit her Justin boots exactly right and showed off her baby bump. Her hair was pulled back off her face and caressed her shoulders and back. She looked prettier than a full moon in a black sky, especially with her sweet belly filling out the front of her dress.

He had to admit that he loved watching her, loved the curve of her face, and the way that ruby hair of hers looked like crimson silk in the sun's evening glow. He loved the lilt of her voice, the smile on her lips, but most of all he loved her fiery ways. He recalled how when they were in first grade together, on one exceptionally cold day when he was trying his best to keep warm out in the school yard, she'd flung a snowball at him that nearly knocked him silly. All his friends made fun of him for not lobbing one back, but he knew even then he'd never win the battle. She always could take aim and hit her mark, probably why she was so dang good at shooting while on horseback.

Back then, he'd admired her arm.

Now he admired her downright audacity.

WHEN HELEN ENTERED the cinnamon-scented lobby she spotted Travis and Gavin in the dining room, mulling around a long table set with fine china and white linen. She hesitated near the oak front desk, speculating about what they were doing inside the inn instead of picking pumpkins with everyone else.

June Butler, Pauline's oldest daughter, looked up from behind the desk and smiled, revealing her beautifully whitened teeth. She figured those pearly whites must be due to Colt's brother Doc Blake and his expert hands. He was the town's only pediatric dentist but most grown women didn't want to give him up just because they were over eighteen. They'd get a crush on him when they were young, and couldn't seem to get over it when they grew into women.

"Did you need something, Helen?" she asked in a sweet, helpful voice.

"Yes, a bathroom."

June pointed the way and Helen took care of business. Ten minutes later, she was coming back through the lobby when Gavin ran out of the empty dining room, boots pounding across the wooden floor, weaving in between the overstuffed chairs and sofa, hair combed neatly to one side, wearing new jeans and a crisp green shirt while he smiled from ear to ear. It was the first time she'd seen him so animated in days.

"Are you in on the secret, too?" he asked, his breath hitching with excitement.

He caught her completely off guard and she didn't quite know how to react. "I, um, no, but if you tell me what it is, I won't tell anyone."

Travis came wandering out of the dining room behind him, grinning at Helen. Gavin turned to his uncle. "Can I tell her, please? I'm all itchy and I can't stand it."

He scratched his belly and his neck and wiggled his lower body. He looked so cute Helen wanted to take him in her arms and give him a tight hug. Despite knowing he was a handful, she'd grown to love this little guy. She loved all three of Colt's boys more than she ever thought possible.

"Sure. It won't be a secret for very long now, anyway," Travis said as he nodded and gazed at Helen. He wore one of those sly little grins all the Granger brothers shared.

"I'll go check on the family," he said and moseyed out the front door, leaving her alone with Gavin.

"Grandpa asked Mrs. Abernathy to marry him, and she said yes. Now we're having a party to celebrate it right over there in that room." He turned and pointed, then turned back to Helen. "The dessert looks like a great big pumpkin, but don't let it fool ya, 'cause Pauline told me it has chocolate cake inside. She didn't tell me how she got it in there, but it looks real good."

Helen was taken by complete surprise. Edith and Dodge were getting married? She had no clue about that one. She wondered how they ever managed to keep it a secret.

"And I suppose the party is starting soon?"

He nodded. "Just as soon as Grandpa can round everybody up."

"That may take a while. Did you pick out your pumpkin?"

"Not yet. I can't find the one I want. Did you pick yours?"

She shook her head. "No. Maybe we could look for them together after the dinner."

"You'd do that with me?"

"Of course I would. Why would you think I wouldn't?"

He gazed down at the floor. "Because I get into a lot of trouble all the time. I don't mean to, honest." He shrugged. "It just sorta happens."

"Let me tell you a secret. When I was your age I used to get into a lot of trouble, as well."

"You did?"

"Yes. One time I accidentally spilled a whole bottle of bleach into the washer with all my school clothes and they were ruined. My mom had to buy me an entire new wardrobe."

"I bet she was real mad."

"She was, but something good came out of it. I didn't like those other clothes anyway. They belonged to some of my cousins and they were all too big."

"Did some of them belong to Milo?"

She laughed. "As a matter of fact, yes, some of them did."

He leaned in closer. "I would've spilled the bleach, too."

She tickled his belly. "You're such a little rascal."

And she couldn't help but laugh some more.

"I'm glad you're going to be our new mother. You're fun."

The statement took Helen by surprise.

"Whatever gave you that idea? Your dad and I aren't getting married."

His little face wrinkled. "Why? Did he do something bad?"

With his question, her heart broke into a million

pieces. "Your dad could never do anything bad. He's the nicest, most honest man I know."

"Then why won't you marry him?"

"We're not ready to get married. Besides, he hasn't asked me to."

He was clearly thinking about that as he tilted his head to one side and said, "But if he asked, would you?"

"Getting married is a big step. I'd have to think about it first."

"Could you think fast?"

Helen believed she and Colt weren't anywhere near seriously thinking about getting married, so she was pretty safe answering Gavin's question.

"Sure. If your dad asks me to marry him, I'll give him an answer right away."

"Sweet!"

"But all this talk of marriage has to be our secret, okay?"

"I won't tell anybody, I promise. But he better ask you pretty soon, 'cause I can't be trusted with a secret for too long. It makes me itchy."

And as he said it, the double doors opened and the entire Granger clan walked in sounding as if the party had already begun. Their voices filled the room as the kids squealed and ran into the dining room, boots pounding on the wooden floor and reverberating off the walls. The Grangers certainly were a dominant presence and she was thrilled she would soon be part of the family.

Helen spotted Colt in the back of the group, holding on to Scout's hand. Blake, Maggie, Dodge and Mrs. Abernathy filed past Helen in a rush of excitement. When Colt let go of Scout, the girl hurried into the dining room in an explosion of excitement, her pink cowgirl boots clicking on the floor. Scout rarely went anywhere without her pink boots. Helen preferred tan, black or grey, even for a child, especially a girl. She never could understand the attraction some little girls had to pink. When she was a kid, she liked black or maybe a touch of purple, but never pink.

Colt came up to her and took her hand in his. "Sorry. We'll have to plan for a talk later," he whispered.

"I've learned there are no set plans with this family," she told him with a chuckle as they took their seats at the end of the table, across from Dodge and Mrs. Abernathy. Colt's boys sat at the far end with Scout.

Colt leaned in and said, "Sorry about that."

She threw him a smile as two male waiters poured red wine in everyone's glass. The kids already had apple cider sitting in short, round glasses in front of each of them and Helen asked for her own apple cider. The taller of the two waiters was quick to fill Helen's order then disappeared through the kitchen door.

Once everyone had a drink in front of them, Dodge stood as Mrs. Abernathy clinked her glass with a spoon for everyone's attention.

"I s'pose some of you know this already, but I'm thinkin' some of you don't. Either way, I thought this here pumpkin pickin' night was a good time to announce that Edith and me's come to a place in our lives when we don't want to be sleepin' in two different houses no more. I've asked her to marry me, and to my doggone bewilderment, she said yes."

The group erupted with hoots and whistles as Dodge held up his glass. "Now if ya'll join me in a toast to this fine woman, I'd be mighty pleased."

Everyone held up their glasses. "To Edith, who's made this ol' cowpoke happier than he's been in a very long time."

"To Edith," everyone repeated as they chuckled at Dodge's folksiness and clinked glasses.

Blake stood up, glass in hand. "To Dodge and Edith. May they have a truly happy life together. May the road always be easy, and may your problems be few. Welcome to the family, Edith."

Again, everyone toasted.

Then Dodge held up his glass again. "And I want Helen to know, that no matter what she and Colt decide to do about makin' their own marryin' announcement, or not, she and my new grandbaby will always have a place in this family."

Glasses clinked, and cheers went up. Gavin twitched and scratched his arms, but didn't say a word. Helen winked over at him, smiling. He winked back, beaming, just as his meal was served. Once all the plates were on the table, everyone held hands and Dodge said a prayer of thanks for this night and his family.

Colt laced his fingers through Helen's under the table and for the first time since she'd learned she was pregnant, a rush of pure joy washed over her. She was filled with love, not only for her sweet baby, but for everyone at the table, including Colt. If he asked her to marry him at that very moment, she was sure the answer would be yes.

But instead, he let her hand go, picked up his fork and the moment was gone, leaving Helen to wonder if she truly loved him or were her hormones playing tricks on her again.

Either way, she knew for a fact, her life would never be the same.

Chapter Eight

"I don't really want to know," Helen said to Doctor Guru as they watched her tiny baby suck its thumb on the monitor.

Everyone wanted an answer to the question: Is it a boy or a girl? Presumably so they could buy gifts for the baby in the appropriate colors. She had assumed it to be a boy and was good with that assumption, but her family kept hinting that they'd love to know for sure. Even Edith had said she thought it was a boy because she seemed to be carrying him so low. Whatever that meant.

"That's fine. We can keep it that way if you'd like."

Problem was, the more Helen watched her sweet baby move around, the more she suddenly wanted to know, needed to know if this munchkin was indeed a boy.

"Wait." She took a deep breath and slowly let it out. "I want to know. Boy or girl?"

The good doctor grinned. "You and Colt are parents of a perfect baby girl."

Doctor Guru practiced both in Jackson and in Briggs. She'd been Kendra's doctor and Maggie's sister, Kitty's, doctor and therefore Helen had always had the utmost faith in her. Now she wasn't so sure. Obviously, the woman couldn't see what had to be right in front of her on the monitor.

"No offense, but aren't you missing something on him? Maybe it's just too small to detect." Helen squinted at the monitor and could make out a head and fingers but little else.

"Trust me. I've been looking at this baby for months now and there is no something. You're carrying a girl."

"But all Colt's children are boys. Colt is one of three brothers. Blake can make girls, not Colt."

Doctor Guru shrugged. "Then consider this a blessing."

"But I don't want a blessing. I want a boy. I don't know the first thing about girls."

"Sorry. Maybe next time."

"There won't be a next time. Colt had a vasectomy."

"And how's that working out for you two?"

"Now's not the time for levity. I'm in a crisis."

Helen's breathing suddenly increased and her fingers were beginning to tingle.

"You're a girl. I think you understand yourself quite well. I've seen you ride and compete. You're incredible. Your daughter will probably develop a love of horses and riding just like her mom."

"My daughter? I don't even have a girl's name picked out. I was thinking of naming him Loren, after my father. Now what do I do?"

"Change the spelling."

What bothered Helen most was that she had to hear this startling news without Colt. He was busy with some real estate deal and couldn't change his meeting. Doctor Guru's staff had tried to move things around so they could be together for her last ultrasound, but it wouldn't work out in their favor. Ironically, she and Milo had been working on their own bid for the old M & M Riding School—something she hadn't told Colt about yet and hadn't wanted to until they were actually ready to put in the offer.

"Colt's been thinking all along this is another boy."

Doctor Guru printed out the pictures of Helen's baby girl, placed them on the counter, then wiped the gel off Helen's stomach she'd lathered on for the ultrasound. The good doctor was a petite Indian woman, with shoulder-length hair, creamy dark skin, and in her early forties, Helen guessed. She exuded confidence behind a friendly smile. Her long last name had defied pronunciation for anyone who hadn't grown up in her culture, so everyone else referred to her as Doctor Guru.

"I'm sure he'll be thrilled with the news. Those boys of his are a handful. I was in the audience at the piglet races this year. A girl in the mix might soften them up a bit."

Helen knew that Colt always had a soft spot for Scout and would probably take to his own little girl like any happy papa and would end up worrying like crazy every time she went out on a date.

It was Helen who was petrified of raising a girl. All this time she'd just assumed it would be another boy. A boy just like Gavin or Joey or even Buddy—whose antics were even known to her doctor.

Scout was definitely more of a challenge, especially now that she'd embraced her feminine side ever since Maggie and Blake had gotten married.

Doctor Guru turned off the monitor. "You can sit up now, Helen."

Helen mindlessly sat up, and rubbed her belly. "A little girl. I don't know where to begin."

"Buy something pink."

"I don't like pink. It's too feminine."

Doctor Guru looked at her. "Have you taken a look in the mirror lately?"

Helen instantly reached up and touched the hair band she'd stuck in her hair right before she'd left the house. The hair band she'd seen in the window of Femme Fatale's and had to own. The pink hair band that she absolutely loved.

"See you in two weeks," Doctor Guru said, a warm smile creasing her lips, as she left the room.

Helen slipped off the examination table and grabbed the pictures of her baby daughter.

This time she could make out her head, and a hand with all its fingers.

"Look at you." Helen ran her finger over her baby's tiny shape. "All curled up and tiny. So, you're a girl. And what a girl you'll be with three brothers to contend with. It's you and me, kiddo. We'll just have to learn how to stick together. You're special, you know that? Now I won't be alone in a family of boys. And, don't tell anybody, but I'm beginning to really like pink."

"A GIRL?"

"That's what the doctor said."

"Well, I'll be." Colt leaned back in his chair looking particularly sexy with his messy hair sweeping across his forehead, and those incredibly blue eyes of his heavy with amusement.

"Who woulda thought I'd be father to a daughter. I figured for sure I could only produce boys."

They were sitting across from each other finishing up dinner, takeout from Wok n Roll, a Chinese restaurant in downtown Briggs. Colt's tiny dining room barely held the round wooden table that his brother Travis had made as a wedding present almost ten years ago. Colt still kept it in good condition, only now there was always a cream-colored tablecloth draped over the top.

For the most part, the house was decorated in masculine contemporary, with very little frill, if any. Most of his deceased wife's things had been stored in the attic, and Helen appreciated that. Colt wanted to keep her memory alive for his boys, but Helen also understood the importance of how she was going to fit into all of this.

Sitting at the table with Colt was awkward enough, she would never want to try to take his wife's place with Colt's boys. The precise reason why she thought starting over at the M & M Riding School would be the perfect solution for them.

If she and Colt ever had the chance of being together, she could never move into this house; he'd have to move into the house at the riding school. Somehow, looking around his house, the family photos hanging on the walls, a fire roaring in the rustic hearth, and seeing Colt sitting at his table, surrounded by everything familiar, that notion seemed next to impossible.

"Are you happy?" she asked, feeling somewhat concerned.

He stood and walked over to her. He took her hand as she stood, then pulled her in close. "Am I happy? Sweetheart, I thought I never wanted another child, thought I was saving a woman from going through a pregnancy, saving myself from the worry. Then I find out that's not true. I'm going to be a daddy. Again. Yeah, it took this bullheaded cowboy a while to come to terms, but once I did, I was very happy. Still am. Now you tell me you're carrying a baby girl. Am I happy?" He wrapped his arms around her. "Darlin', I don't know if I can take any more happiness. It's as if my heart's going to explode from it being filled to the brim."

He gazed into her eyes. "But what about you? Are you happy?"

She let out a sigh of relief that seemed to originate from her toes. "I can't say I'm unhappy. Another girl in the family is exactly what you Grangers need. So yes, I'm over the moon happy about our little girl. I may not know how to relate to her, but I'll learn."

Then he kissed her and it was filled with passion and desire.

Before she could catch her breath they were tugging at each other's clothes and heading for the leather sofa in the living room, which would have been perfect, except that she was way too pregnant to make love on a sofa. Her lower back was already giving her problems. That lumpy sofa would only make it worse.

She angled him toward the bedroom, and once again he moved her toward the sofa.

She had no choice but to come out and tell him. "Can we do this on the bed? My body needs a little more comfort than what your sofa can give me."

"The bed's not made," he whispered as he gently pulled off her top and continued to guide her toward the living room, her round belly now more prominent than her breasts.

"Don't be silly. I don't care about the sheets," she told him as she undid his belt buckle.

"The room's a mess. Clothes all over. Joey and Gavin slept in there with me last night." He sat on the sofa and pulled off his boots.

She sat on the chair across from him and pulled hers off, as well. "Why would I care about their clothes? It's the bed I want."

He walked over to her, his chest looking positively ripped from all the work on the ranch, his pants now unzipped and hanging open from the heavy belt buckle and revealing a trail of fine hair. He looked so inviting she could barely stay away from him for even the time it took her to undress.

"We're here now," he whispered before he kissed her again, his tongue pressing against hers, sending chills over her body. She was ready to make love on the floor, but the whole avoidance of the bedroom was now bugging her.

She pulled away from his grasp and hustled into his bedroom, laughing at the absurdity of his worry over a messy bedroom. As if that mattered.

When she arrived at the open doorway, she saw that the bed was perfectly made and everything was in meticulous order. No clothes on the floor or anywhere else for that matter. No toys. No books. No cars or balls or games.

Nothing was out of place, including the eight-by-ten glossy of a smiling Colt and his deceased wife on the nightstand.

HELEN HAD TRIED to leave, had put her stretchy shirt back on, slipped into her boots and pulled her coat over her arms and buttoned it up tight, but fortunately Colt had sweet-talked her into staying. He'd convinced her he had a reason why the picture was on his nightstand, and a darn good one, so she reluctantly made her way back into the living room. She plopped down on his sofa, looking as if this was a temporary condition and she could leave at any moment. Her coat stayed on, buttoned up tight, along with a dark blue scarf she wrapped around her neck for extra protection.

"It's been four years, Colt."

He attempted to hold her, but she would have none of it and shrugged him away.

"I've tried several times to take that picture down, but every time I do Buddy makes such a fuss that I have no choice but to put it back up."

"Can't you just give *him* the picture? Wouldn't he like it next to his bed? I mean I certainly understand his grief over the loss of his mom. I miss my mom every day, but—"

"That's the problem." Colt sat on the floor in front of her, crossed his legs and looked up at her. She had that glow pregnant women had, as if they were lit from within. She never looked more beautiful. "I won't lie to you. Buddy's not handling all of this very well. He won't talk about it, and he won't let me take down that picture."

"Maybe he needs counseling."

"I took him for grief counseling right after his mom passed, but it didn't seem to help so after a year I stopped taking him. He seemed to come out of his depression after that and had been fine up until I told him about this baby. Ever since that night, he's been moody and I can't seem to bring him out of it. The picture appeared on my nightstand the next morning and I've been apprehensive about talking to him about it. I'd hoped the more he gets used to having you here and us talking about the baby, that he'd come around." He leaned forward, trying to get closer to her, and this time she didn't move away.

"You could've told me about Buddy's difficulties in dealing with this. I'm sure he loved his mother very much and he's scared I might be taking her place. Obviously, he doesn't want me to or that picture wouldn't have shown up on your nightstand."

"I'm sorry. Really, I am. And if I was in possession of even half a brain, I would have hidden it. But I honestly didn't think about that darn picture until we were heading for the bedroom. Then all I could think of was how to keep you out here. Just know that no matter what my boys want, no matter what pictures are on my nightstand, I'm crazy about you, and nothing's going to stop those feelings."

She sat there, not saying anything. He had wanted to tell her he was in love with her, pin his heart to his sleeve, propose marriage, but from her nonreaction he was glad he'd held back. Blake had been right to caution him about moving too fast. He needed to take a step back and wait until the timing was perfect.

She unwound her scarf and unbuttoned her coat, sliding it off her shoulders.

"Does this mean you're staying?" he asked, hopeful.

"Yes, but I've got something to say."

He stretched out his legs and body then leaned his head on his hand. The fire felt warm on his back. She moved off the sofa and sat in front of him on the floor.

"Shoot," he said, ready for whatever she wanted to throw at him.

"Everything you said is wonderful. I'm crazy about you as well, and I love your boys and I hope I'll be a good mom to our little girl." She rubbed her belly, smiling. "There's just one issue, and it's a big one. I didn't really focus on it until tonight, sitting in this house, having dinner with you at the table Travis built, talking about the picture on your nightstand. If you and I have any chance of taking this relationship to the next level, I think you should know, I could never be a good mom to your boys in this house. I'd feel as though I was always being compared to their late mom. As a family, we would need to start fresh, where everything's new."

Colt sucked in a breath and let it out slowly, trying to

dismiss the knot that was forming in his stomach. He didn't want to believe she was telling him that in order for the two of them to make a go of it he would have to move out of his house. He figured she must have something else in mind, some room additions, perhaps, or a complete revamp of the interior. He would do either one of those in a heartbeat. The house needed some improvements, needed some upgrades, but he was not about to consider moving out of it. She had to know how much this house meant to him. He loved his house. His land. The ranch. He and his brothers had built this house on the fork of the river in order to make use of all the sunshine he could get. He and Dodge had planned for this house since he was a teen.

It held all his memories.

How could he possibly… "I'm all for starting new. We could add another bedroom or two, and upgrade the kitchen. Put on a new coat of paint to the inside and out. Buy new furniture. Give the place a whole new look. Add a bathroom."

"That's not exactly what I had in mind. With Milo's help, I want to buy the M & M Riding School and open it up again, under a new name of course, along with a few improvements. We can live there."

His stomach did a huge flip and the sweet and sour pork went completely sour.

She continued. "The house on the property is big enough so everyone can have a room of their own and with Travis's help, we can make the kitchen bigger and add a couple bathrooms and maybe a family room. It would be perfect for us. And the best part is that I can teach there. I'm good with kids, boys especially. You are, too. Not that I'm saying you won't still run this place. It's an option for you to consider. I need something that's mine, Colt. Something I can shine at, win at. I'm used to being on the road a lot, but with at least one child I have to raise, I've come to terms with the fact that I won't be able to do that anymore, at least not enough to compete like I used to. The school will fill in that void, that's what I'm hoping for anyway. What do you think?"

He had no problem with her wanting to start her own riding school now instead of later, and needing her own thing to succeed at. Plenty of women were successful at holding down a demanding career and motherhood. But did she have to want to do her own thing on the very piece of land he'd just put a bid on that morning? A bid that he suspected would be accepted? A bid that would bulldoze all the buildings?

He scratched his head, the heat from the fireplace felt as if it was cooking his skin. He moved away from it and sat on the overstuffed chair next to the sofa, wanting desperately to somehow talk her out of this idea.

"It sounds like a lot of work with a baby and potentially three boys to look after."

"Joey will be easy to have around all day until he starts school. And Buddy and Gavin will be in school during the day, and when they're not, they can help out. Buddy will especially love it. I just know he will. And I bet we can get Edith to help out with the baby. We can start out slow with just a few students, and even rent out the arena to riders who want to train during the winter."

He was reeling on the inside while he tried his darnedest to appear calm and rational.

"Maybe you should think about it for a while. Try it on for size, so to speak."

He was stalling, making excuses as panic tightened his throat. He knew he had to come clean and tell her the truth, but telling her required all his courage, and he wasn't so sure he had any at the moment.

"I'm too afraid someone's going to put in a good offer on the property and we might lose it. I want to make an offer as soon as possible. Milo's been a big help. He pulled in all the funds we need for a nice down payment. He'll make a good business partner. He's good with finances. I really want this, Colt. It means a lot to me."

He ran his hand through his hair, completely baffled. He wanted to tell her the truth, but terrible fear of losing all they had kept him from saying the words. He had no idea how she would react to what he'd done and what he wanted to do with that land.

"Someone already did, this morning."

"But how do you know?"

"Because that someone was the Grangers and two other families."

"You put a bid on my riding school without telling me first?"

"Okay, for one thing, it's not your riding school. It belongs to the Miltons. And for another, you told me you weren't ready to open your own school. That you still wanted to compete."

"That was before I fell in love with you."

Her words took him by surprise. "Hold on. You're in love with me?"

"Yes, but that's beside the point right now."

He went and sat across from her on the floor. "No. That *is* the point. This changes everything."

"You're right. It makes things tougher. I want this school because I'm in love with you. I want a home, our home, not the home where your boys were born, but the home where your daughter will be born. That's our home."

"You might be right, but the storage facility is a necessity for my family and two other families in this valley. We've needed a new one for a long time. It's not a risk. It's a smart business decision that's already been made. I can't change that now. I can't take back the offer."

"So you're saying my school is not a good business decision?"

"That's not exactly what I said. Have you put your offer in yet?"

"No, and there's no reason to now."

She slipped her coat back on, and wrapped her scarf around her neck. Colt didn't want her to leave. Not like this.

She stood, walked out of the living room and opened the front door. A blast of snow came swirling in and he knew she'd probably have second thoughts about going out in that if he handled the situation better.

"Please don't go. We finally have a night to ourselves. We'll settle this. It's going to take a bit of negotiating, is all."

She turned and looked at him, sticking her chin out, looking determined to make her opinion known. "It doesn't sound like you can negotiate."

There may have been room to negotiate if he didn't have two other farmers who were in on the deal, but because he did, at this point, there was almost nothing he could do.

He felt as if he was trying to stand on water.

"You're right, but that doesn't mean that you and Milo can't still put in your offer. Then it's up to the Miltons to decide who gets the land."

"But even if I get it, you won't want to leave this house or this land."

"Let's have that discussion when the Miltons make their decision. If I've learned one thing in this relationship, it's not to jump to any conclusions. Okay?"

But she didn't budge. Helen was just as muleheaded as he was and needed more coaxing.

"It's dangerous for you to leave now. The weather's unforgiving, and it's late. You don't want to drive to Milo's house tonight. Sweetheart, we're both used to doing things on our own. That's all changing now and we've got to learn how to work with each other. We both know it won't be easy, but we need to try, so please stay."

He walked over to her and gently slid her hair off her face. "Let me love you. Tonight. In my bed. Tomorrow morning everything will look different. I promise."

"I won't feel any differently in the morning. I won't live here."

"I know you won't, but you can stay here for one night, right?"

Her face lost some of its fire as she gazed up at him. "There's still a matter of that picture in your bedroom."

He immediately walked into his bedroom, claimed the picture off his nightstand, went into Buddy and Gavin's room, placed it on the nightstand between their beds and returned to Helen feeling as if he'd just crossed over some sort of threshold.

"Done. Anything else?"

"I'm hot in this coat and scarf."

She allowed him to slip off her coat and unwrap her scarf from around her neck. He tossed both of them onto the bench next to the door, which he closed.

"Feel better now?"

She nodded.

He kissed her neck, and tickled her earlobe with his tongue. She smelled like gardenias and roses and her skin tasted like honey. She pressed her body up against his, her sweet belly pushing against him.

"I love you," he whispered. "We'll work this out."

Her face tilted up to his, and he brushed her silky cheek with his hand, glad they weren't headed down the road to Milo's house in his pickup.

"I love you, too, Colt."

That was all he needed to hear.

"I have something for you."

He led her back into the living room and handed her a small box wrapped in light blue colored paper that he'd put up on the mantel a few days ago hoping for the right moment.

He knew now was the moment and he handed her the box.

"What's this?"

"Open it and find out."

She tore the paper off the tiny silver ornate box that his mom had kept on her dresser ever since he could remember. Then she opened the top and the simple three-carat ruby ring Dodge had given his mom on their tenth wedding anniversary caught the overhead light. It looked even more lovely than Colt had remembered it.

She sucked in a breath. "It's beautiful, Colt."

"It was my mom's. I had it cleaned and sized for you."

"But how did you know my size?"

"Crystal Glows from Glow Your World Jewelry in town had it on record." He pointed to the ring. "May I?"

She nodded and he plucked the ring from the box, and slipped it on her finger. "Helen Shaw, will you marry this stubborn, backward cowboy who loves you like crazy?"

Her face lit up with a smile that captured his heart as she wrapped her arms around him. "Yes, I'll marry you, even if you are a stubborn, muleheaded cowboy who loves his kids like there's no tomorrow, and would do anything for his family. Colt Lincoln Granger, I wouldn't want to think of my life without you in it."

They kissed; a soft and sweet kiss to begin with, then hard, with urgency, as he pulled her in tighter.

Even though he should have been thinking about how much he wanted her, which he did with a fire that raged through his body, he couldn't help wondering how the heck they were ever going to come to terms.

Chapter Nine

Confusion reigned supreme on her drive back to Milo's and then lingered as she took a seat at his kitchen table. Colt had been called out early about a missing calf so he'd left her a note and snuck out. Just as well. Helen was a mix of emotions.

"Something smells delicious," she said after she took her first sip of hot black tea.

"You're gonna love these," Milo told her as he placed a lacy crepe filled with melted chocolate, swirls of creamy peanut butter and sliced bananas on her plate, then garnished it with a generous dollop of real whipped cream. It looked like more of a dessert than breakfast.

"What's this?"

"It's my favorite chef's favorite lunch. She makes them whenever she needs her spirits lifted or when she wants to celebrate an event. With that fancy new ring on your finger, I'm thinkin' we got ourselves somethin' to celebrate."

"We do." She stared down at her stunning ring and, yes, she did want to celebrate, but there was still a tiny hold on her happiness. "Colt asked me to marry him, and I said yes. This looks wonderful."

He made himself the same plate and took a seat across from her. The small functional room painted a golden-yellow with dark maple cabinets, a dark wooden plank floor and a rustic table was serviceable but way too small. Every room had a rustic cowboy motif going on and the kitchen was no exception. Helen longed for her own place with her own things surrounding her. Living out of a suitcase just didn't have the appeal it once had.

"That's it? One of the biggest moments of your life and that's all I get? I have a feelin' that you're not as happy as you should be about hitchin' up with that cowboy?"

"It's complicated," she said as she scooped up sliced banana and thick chocolate on her fork, and to get the full effect, opened her mouth wide and shoved it in.

It tasted even better than it looked.

"He did right by you."

"I wouldn't have agreed if that were the case."

"Do you love him?"

She put her fork down and grinned. "Something awful, but I don't want to talk about it."

Neither of them spoke for a few minutes, until Milo broke the silence.

"How do you like my crepes?"

"They're amazing! I can't believe you made this."

"I told you, that TV chef is teaching me the tricks of the trade. And I have my own good news."

She put her fork down. "Please tell me."

"I made it to the final round of the show's contest. I'm gonna bust wide open I'm so excited!"

"You did? Congratulations! So what does this mean?"

"It means I've got a good chance of winning. Now I have to send them an essay of why I think I should win in five hundred words or less."

"If you need any help, just let me know."

"Me and Amanda already wrote it. She's an English major, wants to be a writer."

"What kind of writer? Literary or a genre?"

"Horror."

"Little, quirky Amanda?"

"She has a wicked mind…but in a good way. But tell me why you're not floating on a cloud over your engagement."

Helen took two more big bites before she had the courage to tell him about what she and Colt were arguing over. When she finished the sordid tale, he said, "Seems to me you two have some major issues to sift through."

"The easier thing to do would be to back off on the school and let him have it. I could simply go on competing like I planned. At least I know how to win at that one."

"Now don't be hasty, cousin. You got a baby to take care of. I can see Colt's point, but I can also see yours. And seein' as how I want to make *you* happy, I'll have that offer sent over to the Miltons this morning. That way, like Colt said, it's up to the Miltons to decide who gets their land."

"Cousin, you always know how to make me happy."

"I try my best, cousin."

Helen downed the last bite of Milo's wonderful creation. "Could you do one more thing for me?"

"Anything. You name it."

She held out her plate. "Could you give me more, please?"

He chuckled and his round belly bounced. "Comin' right up!"

"She wants to reopen the riding school," Colt told Dodge as they rode together to check on the calf. Travis, who normally took care of the livestock, was busy with a sick pony on the other side of the ranch.

Even though the sun was shining, the air was bitter cold. Colt wore his black beaver fur hat, two shirts, a deep blue bandanna around his neck, a thick wool over-coat, wool gloves and brown suede chaps over his jeans to keep warm. Dodge was dressed in the same manner, except for a brown beaver fur cowboy hat, and black chaps. Mush and Suzie followed alongside them eager to round up some cattle. The dogs loved to work and there was never any shortage of it on the Granger ranch.

"I had a feeling that would be the case," Dodge offered as a toothpick hung from the corner of his mouth. Dodge used to chew tobacco when he was young, but gave it up for Colt's mom soon after they were married. Problem was he never got over the need to chew on something in the morning, so he chewed on a tooth-pick around in his mouth every morning for as long as Colt could remember.

The new snow was about three inches deep with some high drifts. It sparkled with a rainbow of colors in the early morning sun. The long night had been brutally cold and both Colt and Dodge worried they may have lost a calf or two in the drifts with all that frigid wind blowing. At least one calf that they'd been concerned about was missing.

"Why didn't you say something when I was putting this proposal together?"

"I reckon it was your decision, son, not mine."

"But you could have warned me this would cause a rift."

"You're s'posed to know that woman better than me."

Colt gazed over at his dad. "It never occurred to me

that she'd want to take such a big risk now. She told me she wanted to wait until she retired."

Dodge rolled the toothpick to the opposite side of his mouth. "If I recollect proper, she was the only girl in these parts who jumped off that dang barn roof with you in the middle of the night when you two were just newly made teens. Seems like her risk-takin' has always been clear."

It was true. There was one summer when she and her dad were staying at the Gump ranch, right after her mom passed, when she snuck out and rode over to visit Colt in the middle of the night. It had been her idea to jump off the roof and Colt had gone along with it.

"How'd you know about that night? You never mentioned it before and I never told you about it."

"There ain't nothin' I didn't know about you boys. Even when you thought you was getting' away with somethin', I knew about it. If it wasn't gonna kill you or get ya in trouble with the law, I let it happen. That was just my way. Looks like you got a little of that going on with your boys."

"A little." But Colt knew he wasn't quite up to his dad's level. At least not that he was aware of. He could barely keep up with his boys and their homework, much less what they were doing with their free time. He was hoping Helen could help resolve that with him once they were married. Maybe then he could be more like his dad.

Still, Colt couldn't believe his dad knew about that night, and wondered what else the man knew about him. Some of his antics were less than smart, and he wasn't very proud of them, but that night with Helen wasn't like that.

They had snuck out of their houses and spent the entire night in the barn up in the loft, talking about their futures. It was the first time she'd told him about wanting to learn how to be a mounted shooter. Back then it was a new sport and only a handful of men were doing it. He couldn't understand why in the world Helen would want to compete in a man's sport and not stick to barrel racing.

But then Helen never did walk on somebody else's road.

Dodge continued, "Besides, her interest in opening up that school settles her wanderin' nature, givin' it some permanence. A man with three boys and one more on the way can't be asking for much more than that."

"She said yes when I gave her Ma's ring. We're getting married. And it's a girl. Helen's pregnant with a girl."

Dodge smiled and looked over at him. "Well, I'll be. Good news on both counts, son. Evens things out. Didn't know you had it in ya to make a girl baby." And he rode off, heading for the black heifer standing in the drift with her lost calf beside her. The dogs were already rounding up the other heifer and calf.

One thing about Dodge, he always seemed to know the truth of things, and right now the truth was causing Colt to second-guess one of the biggest business decisions of his life.

FOUR DAYS HAD gone by and the Miltons still hadn't made a decision on the sale of their land, which had caused some tension between Colt and Helen. And as if that wasn't enough, the newly engaged couple had decided to wait to be married until after the baby was born. Dodge had other ideas. He figured it was best to have both weddings before little Loran was born. Colt had tried to argue him out of it during dinner on Sunday night, with the notion that they should each have their own weddings, to make each one unique, but in the end, Dodge had a way of making you feel as though his logic was right, so Colt and Helen had agreed.

They were getting married inside the Granger barn, which had been in need of an overhaul for the past couple of years, and the wedding was the perfect reason to give it one. The new floor was getting installed in the next couple of days, and the walls would be primed and painted barn-red as soon as the weather improved. The hayloft was also getting a face-lift as was the outside of the barn, but that couldn't be painted until spring.

Truth be told, Helen thought the double wedding and the party afterward sounded perfect. There were just under two hundred people invited; some relatives, some friends, her riding team, but mostly neighbors. Exactly what she always had envisioned as the perfect wedding, sans the pregnant bride, of course, and by then, she'd be "ready to pop," as Edith had said.

Now, as she stood next to Tater after their secret early morning ride, methodically grooming his winter coat, first with a currycomb, then with a dandy and now with a soft brush, her thoughts drifted to her teammates, who were undoubtedly gearing up for the next season. She really missed them and missed the freedom they represented. She'd mentioned it to Colt a couple times, and each time he took it to mean that she was unhappy, which she wasn't. She merely felt the loss of something that had occupied most of her time for the past ten years.

"I'm sure you miss the road, don't you, boy?" Helen said as her hands brushed and stroked her horse. "I miss the training the most. Don't you? You and I are so out of shape. I bet we couldn't beat out the lowest scoring rider on the board."

Tater whinnied.

"Okay, maybe we're not that bad, but we're close."

The ride had been slowgoing. Helen's belly was big enough that she had to be extra careful when she rode to make sure she centered herself on the saddle. Plus, she really had to keep her rides from Colt or she'd never hear the end of it.

Tater's winter coat was thick and soft, and she'd let his golden mane go without a clipping for months and it too was long and soft from her extended bouts of brushing it with emu oil. It felt therapeutic to her and she knew Tater enjoyed the attention. Dodge knew she was riding, but he never seemed to tell Colt.

"That's something you two gotta work out. Ain't none of my business to get in the middle of that argument. Colt's got his worries that weigh heavy on his shoulders, but you have to do what you think is best," he'd say and go on with his chores as if nothing out of the ordinary was taking place.

Although, lately, with everything she had to plan for, she was lucky if she was able to ride and groom Tater at all.

When she'd started training Tater it had taken months to get him ready for their first mounted shooting exercise. The initial hurdle was getting him used to wearing earplugs. Tater hated anyone touching his ears, let alone shoving something into them. Then she had to get him used to gunshots. She'd started with a pop gun out in a pasture, then eventually she'd shot off her .45 caliber. When he was used to that their next hurdle was the balloons. They spooked him at first and he didn't want them anywhere near him, but when she was finally able to walk him through an entire course of multicolored balloons without him wanting to run, she knew he was ready.

After that, he took to the course and the audience as if he was born to it.

She heard someone call her name from outside the stable, at least she thought someone had, but when she didn't hear another shout, she decided it must be the wind and she'd imagined it. After all, the more she thought about the voice the more she thought it sounded like Sarah Hunter, one of her teammates. But that was impossible. Sarah was down in Arizona practicing for the next season.

"Helen Shaw, are you in here or is that fella of yours lyin' to me?" Sarah yelled from somewhere near the front of the stable.

Helen dropped the brush into the bucket, and moved as fast as she could out of the stall. There, standing in a ray of sunlight, was a vision she didn't think she would ever see in Briggs, Idaho, much less on the Granger ranch. "Sarah? Is that really you?"

"It hasn't been that long, has it?"

"As I live and breathe."

The two women ran to each other and hugged.

Emotion overtook Helen and her eyes watered. "I was just thinking about you. Are you real? Did you step out of a dream? What are you doing in Briggs?"

"Yes, I'm real. At least I think I am, the last time I checked. No, this is no dream. I'm crazy, that's why I came to visit you here. I could be in Arizona right now, where it dipped down to fifty last night, instead of thirty. It's so cold here."

"It warms up later in the day."

"It sure doesn't feel like it. If I didn't know how much

you loved your man, I'd say you were silly for living here. But let me take a look at you."

They pulled apart. Helen encircled her big belly as Sarah ran her hand over it.

"It's a girl." Helen beamed.

"A girl? That's wonderful. You can teach her how to ride and shoot just like her mama. I bet you can't wait."

"I can't."

"Have a name yet?"

"Loran, after my dad, but spelled with an *A*."

"Cute. I bet Colt is thrilled. He seems like such a great guy."

"He is. But why are you here?"

"Your cowboy contacted me a few days ago and invited me out. But can we go inside? I'm freezing out here."

Sarah's normally smooth features were scrunched up as if making faces would somehow guard her from the frigid weather. She wore a thick knit hat over her long auburn hair, and a red down jacket over jeans, and black cowgirl boots. Sarah didn't go anywhere without her boots. She wore them with everything, even under her wedding dress when she married Kyle, another member of the team. Sarah couldn't weigh more than a wet puppy, and towered over Helen by four solid inches. They were as close as thieves, and as different as cornflakes and doughnuts.

"Sure," Helen told her. "Just let me settle Tater and we can go."

"Tater's here?" Sarah asked, a look of elation on her face.

"Don't know how you could've missed him. He's standing right in front of his stall, waiting for you to give him some attention, I'm sure."

Sarah found Tater and did exactly that, to which Tater nudged and loved her right back, then Helen secured him inside his stall, and the two women walked to the main house. A light dusting of snow had fallen and the two women held on to each other as they carefully made their way across the white glistening landscape.

Up the front porch stairs together, they then pounded their feet on the wooden floorboards to knock off all the snow from their boots. As Helen wiped her feet on the coarse rug just outside the door, Sarah stepped inside with Helen right behind her.

It was at that exact moment when the rest of Helen's riding team seemed to appear out of nowhere, shouting, "Surprise!"

COLT WATCHED AS Helen entered his dad's house, looking completely shocked over seeing all her teammates once again. It warmed Colt's heart to see the wide smile on her sweet lips and the tears that rolled down her cheeks.

He told himself that he'd done good. She needed this now more than ever.

Helen had told him more than once how much she missed her team, and each time, he knew he needed to do something about it. He'd started by contacting her friend Sarah, who instantly helped devise a surprise plan. The few days had been tough for Colt to keep everything a secret, especially from his boys, who would have told her in a heartbeat. And every time Sarah would text or call him he was sure he'd slip up and say something in front of Helen, but somehow nothing like that happened and now there she was, all teary-eyed and excited over seeing her teammates.

"I can't believe it," Helen said once she regained some composure. Colt gave her a little wave from the back of the room, and she threw him a look that told him she was at once happy and angry that he'd been able to pull it off without letting her know anything about it.

He winked back.

"But how did you guys… I had absolutely no idea," Helen told the group as she and Sarah pulled off their coats, gloves and hats, then hung them on the hooks near the front door.

Colt stood by Helen and took her hand while the group of mostly cowboys encircled her, everyone talking at once, telling her how great she looked. Colt knew it was exactly what she needed to hear.

"Colt called me. Said you needed cheering up so I gathered up all these polecats and here we are," Sarah told her. "Brought you a couple gifts from your registry."

She pointed to the mountain of wrapped boxes and gift bags stacked on the coffee table and sofa in the living room.

"Gosh, you guys. That's more than a couple! Wow! I can't believe y'all made the trek out here when you could be basking in the Arizona sunshine," Helen said and her eyes watered once again. This time Colt handed her his handkerchief, then gave her a tight hug.

There were five men and two other women who belonged to Helen's team, all riders who trained, critiqued and encouraged each other. Colt had to admit, he was always a little jealous of Helen's lifestyle and, now, meeting everybody only solidified that jealousy. He completely understood why she missed them so much. They were like a bunch of jaybirds flying together across the sky, all aiming for the same cornfield.

"We couldn't leave our best competitor out in the cold," Sarah said. "No pun intended."

Helen smiled. "I heard you racked up enough points to give me a run for that buckle."

Colt figured Helen must have kept up with everyone's points online.

"You're still way out ahead of me. And you haven't been competing for months. By the time you come back, though, I might be giving you some heavy competition."

"Keep those guns loaded, girlfriend, 'cause once I can compete again, nothing's going to stop me!"

Colt held her hand tighter, almost as if she was leaving now and he didn't want her to go. He didn't understand what she could be thinking. With four children to raise, a house to run, when would she ever find time to compete? Dodge had been right, about the riding school. What on earth had he done by putting an offer on that land for a storage facility? He should have been putting in a bid to buy it for Helen.

Well, there was nothing he could do about it now, but wait for the Miltons to decide.

He didn't want to dwell on what he should have done so instead he decided to get in on the fun. Besides, Helen was better than any of these guys, even Sarah, her biggest competition.

"She can outshoot and outride anybody in this room with one hand tied behind her back," Colt told them.

"You have a lot of confidence in your woman," Sarah said.

"And then some."

The room erupted in hoots and whistles.

Helen was beaming as she leaned into him and squeezed his hand tighter.

He was trying to show support even though on the inside he knew there was no way he wanted her to go back out on the road.

"Food's on the table if anybody cares," Dodge announced.

Seemingly everyone cared because there was no hesitation about getting to the table to eat. As her friends headed for the dining room, Helen and Colt lagged behind.

"Thanks for this," she whispered to him as they took their time before joining everyone else.

"You're welcome, sweetheart. I figured you could use some cheering up."

"I'm fine. Really," she said, but Colt knew better. "Did you meet everybody?"

He nodded. "Now don't worry about me. Just enjoy the afternoon. The boys and Scout don't get home from school for another three hours, and Joey's busy at an indoor park with Maggie. So this house is all yours at least until those kids charging in here looking for warm cookies and milk from Dodge. That should be plenty of time for you to get reacquainted."

She leaned in and kissed him on the cheek. "Did I happen to tell you today how much I love you?"

"Always nice to hear, darlin'. Always."

She took a seat at the table between Sarah and her husband, Kyle, a tall guy who seemed to like black. Not only were his clothes, boots, belt and hat black, but his hair was black, as well.

Colt sat at the far end of the table, next to Dodge. Mush and Suzie didn't budge from their warm spots in the living room, on their beds looking out of the windows, waiting for the kids to come home. Usually whenever Dodge sat at the table, the dogs sat at his feet. Apparently they didn't like all the strangers, so they stayed put.

"We've been thinking of taking on a new member for

our team," one girl said. If Colt remembered correctly, her name was Dale Brown, a slim girl with a sharp-edged face who looked a bit too intense for this group of good ol' boys. "Her name is Vida and she rides a black quarter horse named Rosie, who's almost as fast as Tater."

Colt thought about what a team meant to a mounted shooter, and he remembered that the team was both the rider and the horse. They each racked up points, so they both had to be good at what they did.

"Why? Are you thinking I won't be coming back?" Helen sounded defensive.

Everyone assured her they never thought that for a minute, but Colt could tell from the look on Helen's face that she wasn't buying it.

"We thought it was time to expand our group, is all. Besides, she's one hell of a shooter. She's from Cody, Wyoming," Sarah said. "Her daddy used to rodeo with Kyle's daddy, and he asked if we would consider taking her on."

"Is everybody okay with that?"

Her teammates nodded and said yes in between putting their sandwiches together on their plates or spooning on potato salad, and grabbing handfuls of homemade potato chips. Dodge's specialty.

"And we were thinking that if you had the time…" Sarah said, hesitating for a moment.

"What? I could train them?"

"She's in Jackson, and we thought you might be able to take a peek. Give her some pointers," Kyle said. His voice deep, sounding like a country singer. "But only if you feel up to it, Helen."

Without even blinking, Helen replied, "I'd be happy to."

"Would tomorrow be too soon?" Kyle asked.

"Tomorrow's fine," Helen said, but Colt knew she and Maggie had made plans to look for her wedding dress, and he'd made an appointment for them to fill out all the paperwork at the hospital early in the afternoon. Not to mention the next evening was their introductory Lamaze class.

He didn't know exactly what she was thinking by agreeing to help train the new team member when she was already aware of how he felt about her being around Tater, much less a horse she wasn't familiar with. But whatever it was, he knew there was nothing he could do to stop her.

Chapter Ten

Helen awoke the next morning in the Granger guest room with a start. Her cell phone pinged telling her she had a text. The phone sat on the nightstand next to her bed and she could barely remember where she was let alone how to retrieve the text. She had fallen asleep at seven-thirty the previous night after everyone had left and awakened five times to use the bathroom in the middle of the night, a record of some sort, she was sure.

When she looked at the small screen on her phone, the time registered at eleven-sixteen. She'd never slept this many hours in her entire life. How was that even possible?

She had missed two messages from Maggie, and one from Vida, the new team member. Plus, she had several text messages from Colt reminding her that they had to sign paperwork at the hospital at noon.

She started to answer Colt's text when there was a light rap on the door.

"Come in," she said, not moving.

The door slowly opened and she saw two small feet wearing scuffed tan cowboy boots walk into her room. She instantly sat up and saw Buddy coming toward her carrying a tray of food, looking all serious as he cautiously took each step, trying his hardest not to spill anything.

"Grandpa made you breakfast and asked me to bring it in to you," he said as polite as she'd ever heard him.

She quickly brushed her hair out of her eyes and scooted herself up against the headboard, draping the blankets across her lap.

"Thanks, but how did he know I'd be awake?"

He shrugged. "Gramps just knows."

He ever so carefully placed the tray over her lap, making sure the wooden legs were on either side of her body.

"It looks wonderful."

A plate of Dodge's famous flapjacks was surrounded by scrambled eggs, crispy bacon and blueberries he'd thawed, probably remembering they were a favorite of hers. A white cloth napkin sat under a yellow pot of hot water, with an assortment of tea bags, a tiny bowl of sugar and a delicate pitcher of milk to accompany it. A small stuffed teddy bear dominated the tray, wearing a pink scarf with tiny roses cascading down the front of it.

"I added the bear," Buddy said, beaming. "You can keep it if you want to."

"Thank you. Can I give it to baby Loran?"

He nodded. "It can be her present. I won it at Pia's Pizza Parlor just before that kid and Gavin got stuck in the machine."

"That makes it even more special. It's her very first gift from one of her brothers."

He nodded and turned to leave.

"I have plenty of food here, Buddy, would you like to join me?"

He rubbed his tummy. "My stomach isn't feeling good. That's why I stayed home from school today."

"Then how about some tea? It always makes my stomach feel better and I get stomachaches all the time."

She was hoping she could get him to open up to her. She poured some hot water into the cup then added a mint-flavored herbal tea bag.

"You do?"

"Yep, and my back sometimes hurts and I'm usually tired."

"That's because of the baby."

She smiled. "Do you think so?"

"Ah-huh. You should take a nap every day. That'll make you feel better. My mom used to take a nap with me and Gavin every day when she was going to have Joey and she said it was the only thing that got her through it."

Helen had to force herself to hold back the emotion that gripped her. "If you think it would help, maybe we could both take a nap this afternoon."

"Okay, but we should do it before everybody gets home from school because you can't take a good nap once they come home."

"Why's that?"

He rolled his eyes and sat on the bed across from her. She handed him the tea, and he blew on it then took a sip.

"Because they make too much noise. Haven't you ever been here when we get home from school?"

"No, should I be?"

He giggled, holding his hand in front of his mouth, and Helen saw Colt in his blue eyes. He had the exact same bone structure as his dad, the same sandy hair color and some of the same mannerisms. It was uncanny. "Well, yeah, especially if you're going to be living with us. We're a handful."

"Who told you that?"

He shrugged. "Most everybody."

"Then I have my work cut out for me, don't I?"

"You sure do. My mom used to say that Gavin and me were enough to give her a heart attack. I think that's why she died. We gave her a heart attack. We don't mean to be ornery, it just sorta happens."

She could barely contain the love that swelled for this sweet boy. "Oh, honey. It wasn't your fault or Gavin's fault. Your mama died because it was her time. It's like that for everyone. It had nothing to do with you and your brother."

"Are you sure?"

"I promise. Plus, I know she's watching over you and your brothers every day. She never really left. Nobody does. We just take on a different form. Like when you feel a warm breeze on your face, those are your mama's kisses."

He smiled and his little eyes lit up. "I feel that a lot, especially in the summer, and sometimes in the winter when I first walk in Grandpa's house."

He took several big gulps of his now cooled tea.

"I've felt it, too. And I know it's my mama giving me kisses, as well. There's something wonderful about your grandpa's house, isn't there?"

"Did your mama die, too?"

"Yes. When I was a teenager."

"I bet you were really sad."

"I was. It took me a long time to feel happy again. But I'm happy now being with you and your dad and your brothers and waiting for baby Loran to be born. It's a happy time for all of us."

"Do you think your mama and mine are happy in heaven?"

"Absolutely."

He gazed down at Helen's tray, eyeing those flapjacks.

Helen said, "How about if you run in the kitchen and get us another fork and we share all this. It's too much food for me. Then afterward, let's sneak out for a ride. Tater would love it, and so would I."

"Really?"

"Really. You can ride Kodak. He's as gentle as Tater."

Helen decided spending time with Buddy was more important than wedding plans, signing papers or even training her new teammate. All she wanted to do today was bond with Buddy, the sweetest boy she'd ever known.

He carefully put the cup down on the tray, doing his best not to knock anything over. Then he ran out of the room, returning moments later with another fork and another cup and the two of them sat on the bed talking and laughing as they eagerly devoured everything on the tray.

COLT ARRIVED AT his dad's house expecting to find Buddy lying on the sofa engrossed in some TV show, and Helen just getting up. She'd texted him that she couldn't make it to the hospital to sign the paperwork, saying she felt too tired. At first he'd thought she'd driven off to Jackson to train Vida, but she assured him that wouldn't be happening anytime soon. She was reconsidering whether or not she should do it.

But he didn't find either one of them in the house, which was good. He had news about the land he wanted to share with Dodge and didn't quite know how he was going to do it with Helen in the next room.

Instead he found Dodge alone in the house pulling chocolate chip cookies out of the oven, getting ready for the kids to come home from school.

"I got me a new recipe for these here cookies, thanks to Kitty."

Colt threw him a skeptical look knowing perfectly well that could mean just about anything. Kitty took health food to a new level. "She told you to add raw goat's milk?"

"Nope. I substituted almond flour for some of that there wheat flour. Then I added some rolled oats and used local honey to make 'em sweet. I tried 'em already and you'd never know they were healthy for ya. That Kitty's something when it comes to eatin' healthy. Gotta give her credit for tryin' to keep everybody fit."

Colt grabbed one of the cooled cookies off a plate on the counter and took a bite. They were amazingly good. "Not bad. I've got some news that we need to discuss—first, though, where's Helen and Buddy?"

Dodge slid the cookies off the hot tray and onto a cooling rack. "They're out."

"I can see that. When will they be back?"

"Don't know, son."

Colt knew his dad was avoiding telling him something. "That's not possible. You know everything everybody does in this family."

"Not when it's not my business."

Colt knew this was going to be a guessing game. "Did they drive into town?"

"Son, don't be askin' me where they went. If you and Helen weren't so scared to talk to each other about what's really goin' on, you would know where she is and she'd know you're tryin' to buy her land up from under her. This ain't no way to start a hitch-up."

Colt leaned on the counter. "She knows about my offer on the land. She doesn't know that they countered for ten thousand more."

"This is your chance to do the right thing by her, son."

"You don't realize what that 'right thing' is. If I let her win the counteroffer, she wants me to move off the ranch and live in the house on the Milton land. I don't know if I can do that. This place runs in my blood."

"She ain't asking you to sell the family ranch, she's asking you to start a new life with her somewhere clean. Seems to me it's what your family might be needin'."

Colt's temper flared. He didn't want to hear what his dad thought his family needed. Colt was in charge of these decisions, not his father.

"I know what my family needs and it's not some risky riding school. I worked hard to find the right property for this storage facility and it's the Milton land. It practically borders our ranch. It's centrally located for the other farmers and it's flat. What more could we ask for?"

Dodge looked up at him, his face suddenly stern. "For all your schooling you still don't know nothin' worth a lick."

He threw the empty tray into the sink, pulled off his oven mitts, tossed them on the counter and stalked out of the kitchen. Colt knew better than to press him when he was mad, and he looked madder than a bull staring down a red cape.

BUDDY AND HELEN had spent the afternoon inside the Miltons' arena. She'd been given a key to the place years ago, and the Miltons never bothered to change the locks. The arena was in surprisingly good shape for having been hit by hard times for so long, but then the Miltons always prided themselves on doing things right. Their horses, buildings and grounds were always kept in pristine order, nothing but the best for the M & M Riding School.

But none of that would have mattered if Helen hadn't been able to call Mary Milton and ask permission to come onto the property, which Mary gladly gave her.

Milo phoned a few hours after she and Buddy had been training inside the arena and asked if he could stop by. He had news about their offer and Helen was apprehensive about hearing it.

Certainly she wanted the Miltons to have accepted her offer, but part of her would be sad for Colt, who had done so much work to find exactly the right property for the consortium.

Milo arrived with Amanda, who seemed to be glued to his side. He looked warm and cozy in his bright red parka with the lamb's wool lining and collar. He wore his black hat, black jeans and black boots. Amanda was dressed entirely in creamy-white, from her knit hat, her long wool coat, to her creamy tights and her cream-colored boots. A snow queen if there ever was one.

"Like, this place is ginormous! You could have a rodeo in here," Amanda said as she and Milo walked in holding hands. It was the first time she'd seen Milo show any real connection to Amanda.

Within moments, Amanda went off to cheer on Buddy, who circled the arena riding Tater. When Buddy passed her, his face beamed with pride.

"Hey there, little man," she said to him. "Look at you all cowboy'd up on that good-looking stallion."

"His name is Tater. He's Helen's horse," Buddy told her as he and Tater stopped in front of her.

"Let me see what you can do," Amanda shouted.

Buddy immediately took off, proud to show her what he'd learned.

"She's just a friend?" Helen whispered to Milo as they stood a few feet away from Amanda.

"Okay, so we're a little more'n friends, but that's all. It's not like we're gettin' married or anything."

Helen turned toward the arena. "You're marrying Amanda Fittswater? Get out!"

Milo's face turned bright red as he gazed over at Amanda to see if she'd heard Helen's outburst. Amanda was busy concentrating on Buddy and paid no mind to her or Milo.

"No, and kindly lower your voice." He moved farther away from Amanda. Helen followed. "She's too young to be getting married. I mean, I haven't asked her, yet. No, that's not what I mean."

"Yet? So you really are thinking of marrying Amanda. Cousin, you always amaze me."

He sighed. "You got a way about yourself, little cousin, that jumbles up my thoughts. I'll admit that filly has me flustered. I can't think of nothin' else. Even winning the cooking show contest don't, I mean, doesn't seem to matter."

"What? You won?" Helen gave him a tight hug. "That's fabulous news. I don't believe it."

He grinned and nodded. "Yeah, I won, but I don't want to go anywhere without Amanda."

"Then take her with you."

"I'm afraid to ask her. She's got her classes at the college, and her job, and what if she doesn't like me as much as I like her?"

Helen glanced over at Amanda and at that very moment she turned and looked at Milo, waved, gave him a big wide grin, then looked back at Buddy.

"Believe me, cousin. That girl couldn't love you more if she was hypnotized into it."

"You think so?"

"Definitely. Now go ask her to join you on your adventure. I still can't believe you won. Be happy."

"I am, but you and…I…gotta, I mean, we have to sign these here papers first. The Miltons countered for ten thousand more. I think we should give it to 'em, and maybe a couple thousand more just to make sure we get it. Then I've got somethin' to say that's gonna confuse you as much as it hog-tied me."

"What's wrong?" Helen hated when he tried to keep something from her.

"Let's sign these here papers first, then I'll tell ya."

While Buddy and Tater circled the arena, and Amanda watched, she and Milo sat at a small rickety table to go over the documents, making sure they signed all the pages in the appropriate places. His lawyer had already highlighted where they needed to sign, which made it a lot easier.

Helen didn't understand why they were countering with more than the Miltons wanted considering that Colt wouldn't be countering. He knew how much this place meant to her and what it would mean to their family, so she felt confident she and Milo would be the new owners.

"Look at Buddy," Helen said. "He needs this place. All Colt's boys need this place. I'm sure he'll come around to my way of thinking once I tell him what happened here today."

Buddy had Tater in a brisk canter around the arena. He sat high in the saddle just like Helen had taught him and looked as if he was in complete control. Tater seemed to love Buddy and Buddy took to Tater as if they'd always worked together.

"That means you'll have to tell him you were riding. That's a long ride from the main Granger house to here."

"Two and a half miles if you take the shortcut through the fields, but that's beside the point. Buddy reminded me that I can't give up on who I am. I'm a rider. A competitor. I don't feel whole if I can't have a horse under me or if I can't train somebody else. Look at them. Because of Tater, Buddy and I can relate to each other again. It's what he needs. More important, it's what I need to be a good mother and a good wife. This place is exactly what this family needs." She turned back to Milo. "Let's do it, big cousin."

"Whatever you want."

"When you put in the initial offer was our lawyer able to tell the Miltons that we want to keep it as is?"

"Yeah, although I have a feelin' they don't much care. It's all about who gives them the most money."

"Is there a third party in the running?"

"Nope. Just you and Colt and his counter went in right before I called you."

"Dad! Dad!" Buddy yelled as he burst into Dodge's house, red-faced from running in the cold. Helen followed behind him looking rushed as she watched Buddy run up to Colt. By the time he reached his dad he was completely out of breath. "You won't…believe…what…we did."

Colt knelt on one knee, grabbing Buddy by his arms. "Slow down, son. Take a breath."

Buddy followed orders for a moment and caught his breath. Joey, Gavin and Scout sat around the table doing their homework with Maggie's help. Blake was still in his office with a patient. Dodge was busy in the kitchen cooking dinner with Edith, who now joined him most evenings.

Everyone's attention was now on an obviously well Buddy.

"Dad, you won't believe it, but Helen let me ride Tater today. We rode all the way over to the old riding school and she got us in, Dad. She has her very own key. Can you believe it? Her own key. We had the whole place to ourselves. The whole place!" He opened his arms and walked around in a big circle to demonstrate. "I learned how to go from a canter through a half halt to a gallop then back again. It was great, Dad. He followed all my cues. And Helen said I can ride him whenever I want to, as long as it's okay with you. Is it okay, Dad?"

Dodge walked out of the kitchen. "That's mighty fine, Buddy. Mighty fine."

Colt's gaze went over to Helen, not understanding how she could ride like that when she knew how much he didn't want her to. It was one of the reasons why he took Tater in the first place.

Despite Buddy's enthusiasm, Helen wasn't smiling.

"You and Helen rode all the way over to the riding school and back again?" Colt asked Buddy as anger and fear pushed through his veins.

He nodded. "Yeah, and I wasn't even scared."

Colt wanted to be excited for his boy. Wanted to congratulate him for all that he'd learned but all he could think of was Helen up on that horse out in the elements, crossing fields and a busy street to get to the school.

"What were you thinking?" he said to Helen, ignoring Buddy's excitement. He couldn't focus on Buddy right now. He was too busy picturing Helen getting thrown from her horse.

"But, Dad, aren't you proud of me?" Buddy asked.

"I was thinking your son needed some attention," she said. "What were you thinking when you put a counter bid on *my* school to turn it into a potato storage plant and didn't tell me?"

"But, Dad, what about my learning how to handle Tater? Wasn't that great, Dad?"

"That's really special, Buddy," Mrs. Abernathy said. "Why don't you come on over here." She held out her arm.

"I'll make you some hot chocolate," Maggie said. "You must be cold."

"Since when did it become *your* school?" Colt asked, moving closer to Helen.

"Since I told you I put an offer on it with Milo."

"That doesn't make it yours."

He moved up right next to her, wanting to ask her if she felt all right after that long ride. He was so scared something might have happened to her and so scared that something could still happen to her that he couldn't think of anything else.

"Not yet."

"What does that mean?"

"Milo and I put in a counteroffer this afternoon, just like you did, so once again we'll have to wait and see if it's my school or your potato plant."

"And you didn't tell me? This affects everything."

"So does tearing down that arena and that school and that house. You know how much I love that place."

"And you know how much I love you. How could you ride all the way over there and put our baby in jeopardy, and maybe your life in jeopardy?"

She stared at him hard. "You know I would never do anything that could harm our baby. How could you say those things to me?"

He knew deep in his soul that she was right, but intense fear had gripped him so thoroughly the words coming out of his mouth only served to make things worse instead of speaking from his heart. Suddenly he felt as if he needed to rewind the entire encounter, but he was knee-deep now and there was no turning back.

Silence engulfed them and Colt realized his entire family had disappeared from the room, leaving them alone to deal with this thing on their own.

Before he could get his head on straight again, Helen had slipped off his ring and handed it to him. "Maybe we need to rethink our commitment to each other. Obviously, neither one of us is ready for the truth."

And without really thinking about it he opened his hand and took the ring.

The next thing he knew, the front door had closed and he heard her drive away.

Chapter Eleven

After a sleepless night, complete with pacing, several calls to Helen, who never answered, a couple shots of brandy and a lot of soul-searching, Colt drove over to Milo's house bright and early the next morning, only to learn Helen had driven back to Jackson as soon as the sun came up. He then dropped his boys off at school, left Joey with Edith and drove to his father's house.

He called Travis to join him, along with Blake and Maggie, who had to reschedule all their appointments in order to accommodate Colt's special meeting. When they were all assembled at Dodge's table, and the coffee was poured, Colt made the speech that he'd practiced at two in the morning.

"This was a tough decision for me, perhaps the toughest business decision I've ever made, but I've come to terms with it and I have to follow through." He took a deep breath. "I don't exactly know how to go about doing this. I called our lawyer and she's going to go over all the documentation."

"Get to the point, son," Dodge said, then took a drink of his black coffee.

The men liked their coffee served black in heavy ceramic mugs, while Maggie sipped her creamed coffee from a fine china cup with a saucer.

"The truth is, I can't bulldoze something that means so much to the woman I love more than my own soul. I know it's a big risk, but I'm going to do it anyway." He paused to take a sip of his coffee and catch his breath. He felt hot and sweaty even saying it out loud.

Maggie reached across the table and touched his hand. "Colt, you need to tell us what's on your mind."

"Brother, you sure do take your sweet time getting to a point," Travis said. "You're slower than a snail climbing a greased log."

Blake smiled and nodded toward Travis, who sat back in his chair looking satisfied with himself for saying what everyone had to be thinking.

Colt began again. "Look, I know it's risky for Helen and me to buy that old school and try to run it ourselves, but I discovered something yesterday. I love her and need her to be my wife and the only way I'm going to get her to agree is if I do right by her. So, I put in an offer for the M & M Riding School on my own this morning. I offered five thousand better than what the consortium offered and the lawyer for the Miltons just phoned to tell me I won the bid."

Everyone tried to say something at once, but Colt wouldn't let them until he was finished. "The boys and me will be moving out of my house and into the main house at the school. With some help from Travis I think we can make it livable and Helen has some ideas on how to make it bigger, if she ever forgives me. Anyway, the problem is I'm going to have to cut back on my responsibilities around here, which means we'll need to hire more ranch hands or bring in some of our city cousins who've been itchin' to get their hands dirty on a potato ranch. And the consortium will have to buy that piece of land Travis and I looked at just off Highway 33. The good thing is it's cheaper. Anyway, that's all I have to say on the subject."

Dodge leaned in first. "And when are ya thinking of moving out of your house?"

"As soon as the deal closes."

"Can the deal close before my weddin'?"

Everyone at the table was staring at Dodge, waiting to see what else he had to say on the subject. So far he wasn't making any sense.

"I think it can get done in a week or ten days or so, yes, but there's a lot of paperwork that has to happen between now and then."

"Is the place livable for you and your family?" Travis asked Colt.

"With your help we can make it near about perfect in no time."

"You got it, brother. I'd have to check it out, but no matter what, if we all work together and I can hire some other folks to help, we can fix up a few rooms of that big ol' house to make your family comfortable as kittens on a milk farm."

Dodge had the definitive word on all business negotiations in the family. Always had and this was no different. Colt couldn't imagine what he was thinking. Why did he care if the old schoolhouse was ready in time for his wedding, anyway? No one said a word. Everyone waited on Dodge. He took a swig of his coffee, put the cup down easy and said, "Then this here's how it's gonna be. Edith and me will be movin' into Colt's house after we get hitched. About time Blake and Maggie took over this here house, especially now that they're addin' to the family."

Maggie shot Blake a look. He held up his hands. "What? I didn't say a word."

"Maggie's pregnant?" Travis asked.

"And you didn't tell us?" Colt added.

"We just found out for sure yesterday," Blake said.

"But Dodge knew a couple weeks ago," Maggie explained, turning to Dodge. "Didn't you?"

"A woman shows her glow as soon as that baby's in place," Dodge said. "It's right there on Maggie's face. All ya gotta do is see what you're lookin' at."

"Well, don't that beat all," Travis said, standing to hug Maggie and Blake.

Colt went over and hugged Blake and Maggie, as well.

"So wait a minute," Blake said, putting a stop to all the good wishes. "Dad, you're actually moving out of your house?"

"You boys knew this house would be Blake's someday. Well, instead of me dying in order for you to make it your own, son, I'm getting wed and we'll be needing our own nest, like it should be." He turned to Colt. "I'm glad you finally got your head on straight, son. We'll get through the tangle of paperwork this here decision is gonna make, but now you just gotta show Helen you're serious. She ain't stopped lovin' you. She just stopped lovin' your pigheaded ways. Seems to me, you best be making that place your own sooner rather than later, so we can all start settling in before the deep freeze of winter comes a-callin'. Have you told her yet?"

"She won't answer my calls."

"Did you try going over to Milo's?" Blake asked.

"This morning, but she's back in Jackson with her parents, surrounded by her cousins. She might as well be locked up in Fort Knox for all the chance I have at getting to her."

"Then you have to get Milo on your side and set up a surprise meeting with Helen," Maggie suggested.

"Getting Milo on my side is like spittin' in the wind. He won't pay me no mind. He's dedicated to Helen."

"All the better, son," Dodge said, throwing Colt a wink. "Now let's talk movin' 'cause this family's got a lot of it comin' up."

And he poured everyone another cup of coffee. It was going to be a long day.

TWO FULL WEEKS had gone by since Helen had given back Colt's ring and her anxiety had grown into an all-consuming monster. Not only was she nervous about her fast approaching due date, but the Miltons had long since passed on her counteroffer, which meant her beloved riding school was headed for complete annihilation.

Ever since she'd heard the news she'd gotten restless and could no longer hang around her parents' house knowing Colt was in charge of the school's demise. So instead she'd headed off to the local arena almost every day to train Vida, her new teammate.

Although the training had been fun and spending time with her friends was the shot in the arm she'd needed, her belly had gotten so big she couldn't ride anymore, which made standing around the indoor arena torture. If she couldn't ride, why put herself in the situation? She finally stopped going. Colt would be happy, if he even cared anymore that her days were now spent at home, mostly, reading and nesting. They hadn't spoken since the night she'd returned his ring.

He'd called several times, at least once a day, but she hadn't answered. She thought about returning his calls, or listening to his messages, but then decided not to. Milo told her he'd stopped by a few times, and he'd even stopped by her parents' house in Jackson, but her family wouldn't allow him to come in.

Just as well, they had nothing to say to each other. As long as he was tearing down buildings she couldn't face him.

They seemed to be standing at one of those impossible impasses that would never be resolved and their separation tore at Helen's heart more than she thought possible.

Most of the time, she busied herself with nesting, an act she'd never envisioned for herself. Whenever she'd seen it in other women she would mentally make fun of it, as if decorating and cleaning was all that important. Yet, there she was fussing over her old bedroom: changing the heavy drapes to white sheers to let in more light, asking her dad to paint the walls a light green, buying a new ruffled comforter, scrubbing the floor, moving in the floral rocker she'd bought from the megastore, dusting every inch of the room and finding the absolute perfect location for the cradle Kendra had given her, right next to her bed.

The room shouted girlie-girl and Helen loved it.

She was even planning to repaint the walls in her own house as soon as she could move in, again in pastel colors instead of the tans and whites that dominated the house now. Helen had turned into a nesting mama and she happily embraced every aspect of it.

But nothing seemed to assuage her longing for Colt's touch or the sound of his laughter or his kiss. And she desperately missed his boys despite their hell-raising ways.

As her time grew closer she needed Colt more and more, especially at night when even the comfy body pillow didn't seem to help ease her lower back pain or when her baby had long bouts of hiccups that tended to drive her crazy. She desperately wanted him with her, to have him gently lay his hand on her belly, and tell her how much he loved his girls and assure her everything was going to be all right.

There had been so many times she'd wanted to call Colt and ask him to reconsider, but each time she stopped herself when she thought about his beliefs on taking risks, on moving off the ranch or on his anger over her riding Tater.

She cried when she learned she'd lost the bid, and cried every time she thought about the loss of that perfect arena. She'd been so upset about it that she seriously considered taking Sarah up on her standing offer to teach at her school in Arizona. She could start fresh there. Raise her little girl in open country, surrounded by her riding friends. It might be a good change for her instead of staying in Briggs knowing that Colt didn't love her after all.

Dodge and Edith Abernathy were getting married in two days. It should've been her wedding, as well. She still carried the license in her purse. The sad thing about it was, she couldn't seem to let it go. Couldn't bring herself to tear up the license and move on.

Silly girl.

She tugged at the lapis lazuli necklace she always wore as she walked into Belly Up. She was meeting Milo and Amanda there for dinner. They had news they wanted to share and she hoped it was something wonderful. She needed a good dose of happy.

She tried to dress for the occasion, even though absolutely nothing fit her anymore. In the end, she wore the only pair of maternity jeans that she could pull on, a loose-fitting purple top over a snug-fitting T-shirt, which by itself made her feel like a balloon, and her pink hair band with the little pink bow. For some reason she hated the feeling of her hair on her face, so in the past couple of weeks, whenever her hair wasn't pulled back in a ponytail, she'd worn the girlie hair band.

Soon she spotted Amanda and Milo sitting at a table in the back under the large painting of the round nude who was stretched out on a bright pink velvet chaise with a white fringed shawl, embroidered with tiny hearts, barely covering her privates. There had always been speculation about the identity of the young woman on the chaise, but nothing concrete. Rumor had it that she was a real person who had ties to the original owners of the tavern back in 1955 when it was first opened for business.

"Helen!" Milo called, waving at her.

Helen waved and headed straight for them, looking forward to a tall glass of plain soda water to get rid of her indigestion. When she finally made it to within a few feet of the table she stopped cold. Colt had just walked up to the table carrying a long neck bottle of beer in one hand and what looked like a soda water with three olives in the other.

Her own cousin had set her up.

Chapter Twelve

"Helen. Wait!" Colt called out to her.

But she didn't want to wait, at least not enough to listen to his explanation. Instead she rushed to her car, which she'd parked down the street from the tavern.

"Please, wait up," he yelled, but she kept walking.

Of course, she couldn't walk very fast. It was more of a quick waddle than a fast trot, but she tried her best to make it to her car. She knew if she stopped and listened to him, he'd sweet-talk her into something she'd regret later.

She could hear his footsteps getting closer, until he was right beside her.

"Please talk to me, Helen. You can't avoid me forever. This valley's too small."

She stopped walking and stood under a streetlight to face him. It felt good to gaze into his eyes again.

"Yeah, well maybe I'll move out of this small town. Move someplace where I can see the sky all around me. Somewhere where I don't have to be reminded of our past every day. Don't have to be around a cousin who likes to betray me."

"Milo's a romantic at heart. You know that. Besides, you can't move away from this valley, just like I can't. This soil runs through our veins."

She refused to cry. Refused to let her hormones get the best of her.

"I can move anywhere I want to. I'm a free woman, remember?"

He smiled. "You love it here. You love all the people. This is your home. This is our home."

"It's not *our* home. It's *your* home. It's your family's home. A Granger puts a bid on a piece of land and they get it. No matter what they want to do with it. I thought the Miltons were my friends. But in the end, it was all about dollars and cents. How could I have been so wrong about them? About you?"

Raw emotion began to bubble up inside her. She couldn't stop her eyes from watering no matter how hard she tried. Pregnancy intensified everything, especially this close to her due date.

"Helen, you don't know what's been going on."

She waddled in front of him now. Her car being only steps away she unlocked the doors as she approached, wanting to simply jump in and drive away. She knew if he touched her she wouldn't be able to pull away.

"Oh, I understand all right. I'm a risk taker and you're stable. I'm a wild child and you're responsible. Well, good luck with that. Good luck with your...*potatoes.*"

She went around to the driver's side, opened the door and climbed into the seat. She wished she could do it faster, but getting in and out of a car took effort.

Colt came around to help her. He grabbed her elbow and a shock of heat surged through her body. Her belly even tightened. What was that all about? It scared her for an instant, but she pushed the moment out of her mind and was able to pull her arm away from him.

She finally settled in the seat. Preventing her from

closing the door, he then leaned in, holding on to the door with one hand, the other on the roof of the car.

"I love you, Helen. That hasn't changed." His voice was low and raspy, as if he could barely speak. As if emotion was squeezing the back of his throat.

She looked at him, trying for indifference, feeling anything but. "Don't you have a different line? You've used that one already and I don't believe it anymore."

And she turned forward in her seat, trying to get comfortable, but lately, unless she was surrounded by a mass of pillows, she was chronically uncomfortable.

She hesitated, her hands on the steering wheel, eyes facing forward, wishing he would say something to take her anger away, to convince her that he really did want to work this out.

"I hope you'll be coming to the wedding. Dodge would like it. And my boys would love to see you there and so would I. We miss you, Helen, miss you like crazy," he said.

She wanted to ask him how he could ask her to come to the wedding when it was supposed to be their wedding, as well. She wanted to tell him definitely not.

No way.

Never going to happen.

Instead she looked at him and said, "I miss the boys, too."

Then she forced herself to turn over the ignition, pull the door out of his hand and drive away, leaving him standing in the street watching her taillights fade into darkness.

TWENTY MINUTES LATER, Helen pulled up to the stables at the Granger ranch. She hadn't seen Tater ever since she'd broken off the engagement with Colt. She'd completely neglected her animal and it would serve her right if he didn't recognize her.

She hoped he did, for her own sake.

As soon as she turned on the lights inside the stable, she heard the familiar rustling of the horses inside their box stalls. For some reason, the smell didn't make her nauseous. Instead, it worked like a balm to soothe her ragged nerves. Just seeing Colt again had brought up all her raw emotions. She felt sick over their circumstances and wished with all her heart that the hurt would vanish so they could be together again.

Helen found Tater's stall and peeked inside. Usually whenever she was anywhere near, he would hang his head over the gate to greet her. This time, he stayed back, convincing her that he had forgotten all about her.

"Tater, it's me, boy."

She waited, and slowly he walked toward her. When he finally came closer, he pricked his ears then shied away, taking a couple steps back.

"What's wrong? It's me, boy. Come on. You know me. What's got you so spooked?"

But he wouldn't come to her.

His ears moved again as if he'd heard a noise or seen something that he didn't like. His behavior had her confused especially since this horse was conditioned to hearing guns fire and balloons pop.

Nothing phased Tater.

"How about if I brush you? Maybe that will calm us both down."

She found his soft brush in the bucket she kept stored with all her other favorite brushes and oils at the far end of the stable then made her way back to the stall. She thought she'd take him out and tie him in front of the stall to brush him in order to have more light. Plus, her belly was so big she couldn't really move too quickly if she had to get out of his way.

Helen really missed Colt. It had been so nice sharing her life with him, with his boys and his family. Was their fight over that old school and her secret rides really worth them being apart? What was wrong with starting her own school somewhere else, like say behind Colt's house? Okay, so maybe the house—as it was—was connected to the memory of his deceased wife. She could change that, could paint and remodel. Wasn't a good relationship all about cooperation?

She didn't want this ache in her heart to go on any longer. She loved Colt and he loved her, surely there had to be a way for them to find common ground.

When she reached the stall, she put the bucket down, and was about to slide the gate open when she heard the stable door open.

"I wouldn't be goin' near him, if I was you," Dodge said as he ambled toward her.

Helen's stomach pitched. "Why? What's wrong with my horse?"

"He's got himself an infected tooth. Been jumpy for a couple days now. Doc came by today and fixed him up, but it's gonna take a spell."

She slid the gate partially open. "He's had bad teeth before and he's never been spooked."

Dodge raced over to her just as Tater whinnied and slammed his rear into the back wall, and lifted his front feet, striking a side wall with a heavy hoof. Tater's angry movement frightened Helen, causing her to jump back and lose her footing. She started to go down, but Dodge caught her arm and held tight.

"I got ya," Dodge said.

Helen's balance was so off she couldn't stop her momentum. Dodge struggled to keep both of them upright, twisting his upper body to hold them steady. Somehow he not only managed to keep them upright, but he also managed to keep from hurting her arm when she leaned into him with her full body weight.

"I'm okay. I'm okay," Helen mumbled.

Dodge eased his grip, but didn't let go of her. "You sure you're good?"

"I think so," she told him, but she was shaking so hard she could barely speak. "How about…you?"

He reached out and awkwardly slid the gate on the stall shut with his left arm.

"Think I wrenched my right shoulder, but thankfully, we didn't go down."

"Oh, Dodge. I'm so sorry. I never expected—"

"Ain't nobody's fault. Now, how about you and me go over to the house and set a spell? Blake put the tea kettle on before I walked on over here. Should be hot by now."

She took a deep breath and let it out trying to calm her shaking body, worried about the adrenaline that had to be washing over her baby. Little Loran kept moving and kicking. Helen had never been so scared in her entire life, and now she had a new worry, her sweet baby girl.

"I could use a hot cup of tea…and a slice of humble pie if you've got the time to listen."

"Door's always open, Helen. I'd be mighty proud to serve up some of my own pie, if you don't mind."

"I'd do anything for you, Dodge. You just saved my life."

EXACTLY ONE HOUR before the wedding, Colt helped his dad into a black suit coat then a black sling for his right arm. Colt didn't exactly know how he'd wrenched his shoulder, Dodge wouldn't say, but he knew it had something to do with Tater. He was surprised his dad would've gone near Tater when he knew the animal was hurting. Colt figured his dad's age must be catching up with him and let it go at that.

Travis gave his dad's new hat a once-over, then carefully placed it on his dad's head. Blake made sure his dad's burnt-orange-colored tie had the appropriate knot, and that his hair didn't stick out of his hat in a peculiar way.

Dodge had gotten a haircut special for the occasion. His thick white hair now had a sheen to it due to the rinse his barber had insisted would bring out more of the highlights. Dodge had balked at the idea, but his barber could argue a golfer into climbing a tree. Colt was sure his dad agreed to all the primping and the new suit because both his barber and his tailor had been invited to the wedding along with anyone else Dodge had a mind to tell to stop by. In the end, there were more than three hundred guests waiting for the ceremony to begin in the restored barn. Colt hoped Helen was among them.

"How do I look?" Dodge asked, turning from the freestanding floor mirror that had been their mother's. They were in the master bedroom that would soon belong to Blake and Maggie. Whenever Colt thought about his dad not living in the main house anymore, it made him sad to know it was the end of an era.

But life was about change, and a Granger change had been long overdue.

Dodge looked happy, content and like the true gentleman he was. His best pair of black boots had been polished to a spit shine, his face was clean-shaven, he smelled musky sweet from the cologne Edith had given him and his nails were perfectly manicured. Dodge hadn't looked this good since their mom's funeral, and even then, he'd forgotten to polish his boots.

"Like the handsome groom," Blake said as he fastened a red rose boutonniere to his dad's lapel.

All four of the Granger men had outdone themselves. They each wore black suits, white dress shirts and burnt-orange-colored ties. Their boots were polished and their hats were new. They'd coordinated their suits, shirts and ties and each met Edith's stringent approval. This was her first real wedding, and she was bound and determined that it would be as perfect as a harvest moon.

Her first marriage took place at the courthouse. She and her husband couldn't afford anything else. She told Dodge she'd always felt cheated and this time, she was going to shoot the works, which seemed to be the case if Colt was any judge of what this day was costing.

"I'm nervous, can't fight it," Dodge told his sons.

Colt had never seen his dad so fidgety. Most of the time, it didn't matter what was going on, Dodge was as cool as an ocean breeze.

"It's going to be fine, Pop," Travis told him. "Everything's under control. The preacher's already here, and everyone's gathering in the barn."

"I dismantled the trampoline just in case any of my sons decided to make the leap, and Milo promised to keep an eye out for them. They're too scared of Milo to do anything prickly. You're free to enjoy yourself," Colt said.

"You've-got yourself the perfect day for a wedding, Pop," Travis said. "Not a cloud in the sky, no snow in the forecast and it's a balmy fifty-five degrees out there. Couldn't be better weather if you'd ordered it. Did you?"

Dodge smirked. "I'd like to think I did, son. I couldn't

take it if somethin' went wrong for Edith. She's been plannin' and lookin' forward to this day for weeks."

"Trust me," Blake said, gently slapping his dad's shoulder. "Nothing's going to go wrong."

And as if on cue, Buddy and the dogs, Mush and Suzie, burst into the bedroom. Colt's heart skipped a beat.

"I spoke too soon," Blake said.

"Dad, you gotta come quick." He grabbed his dad's hand and pulled. The dogs barked and Colt had no choice but to follow, hoping like heck this could all get resolved quickly.

"I'm sorry," he called back to his brothers and his dad. "Whatever it is, I'll take care of it. Don't worry."

When they were out on the front porch, Colt said, "I asked you boys to please be good today. This is your grandfather's wedding. He and Edith will be disappointed if any of you get into trouble."

"We didn't get into any trouble, Dad. I promise. This is something good."

The guests were arriving and parking their cars in the empty field that Colt and Travis had prepared for the occasion. There were small bouquets of fall-colored flowers tied to the fence that ran up to the house from the road. The front porch had been cleaned and the wood stained with a dark resin. More fall-colored flowers decorated the porch in huge vases and containers. Cream-colored ribbons and bows wound around the railings and a white plastic runner made its way from the house to the barn. Colt and Buddy sidestepped the carpet as they made their way toward the accumulating guests. Even the dogs knew better than to step on the runner.

"Buddy, I'm supposed to be helping Dodge get ready."

"Gramps is all grown-up. He doesn't need helping,"

Buddy told him without looking back, still tugging on Colt's hand.

When they finally arrived at the front door of the barn, Buddy stopped and looked around. Rows of white chairs lined the new barn floor. Streamers hung from the rafters and an arbor decorated in more fall-colored flowers stood at the back of the barn. All the walls had been painted a deep red and the rafters had been cleaned. The place looked like something right out of one of those magazines his mom used to read.

"She came, Dad. She's here and she's all dressed up looking like a beautiful angel."

And sure enough, Helen stood next to Milo and Amanda, looking exactly like the angel Buddy just described. Her long deep green velvet dress fit perfectly over her round tummy, and her red hair glistened in the sunlight. She wore a floral headband that looked exactly like a small halo. He wanted to walk right over to her, take her by the hand and tell her to stop being so dang stubborn.

But he knew better. "She doesn't want to talk to me, son."

"Sure she does, or she wouldn't have come."

Buddy continued to pull on Colt's hand. This time Colt pulled back. "Buddy, I said she doesn't want to talk to me."

He let go of Buddy's hand and turned to leave.

"But you've got to talk to her, Dad, or Gavin will miss the whole wedding."

Colt stopped dead, and turned to face his son. A combination of apprehension, fear and anger surged through his veins. "Why? Where's Gavin? And where's your brother Joey?"

"Gavin was all twitchy when he saw Helen. We had

no choice, Dad. He made us lock him inside that old hay bin up in the loft so he couldn't tell her about the school. He didn't want to spoil your secret. You have to tell her or Gramps and Edith will never forgive him for missing their wedding."

"You locked him in? With what?"

Buddy shrugged. "The old padlock that hung on the wall up there."

"There's no key for that padlock. Where's Joey?"

"He stayed up there with him 'cause he got scared when we couldn't get the lock open again."

Colt bolted for the ladder to the loft. On his way, he had to pass Helen.

"Colt, I—"

He held her shoulders for a moment and looked into her eyes. She smelled sweet like the flowers she wore in her hair. "I can't talk now, Helen. Gavin's locked inside the hay bin. Please don't go anywhere. You look beautiful, Helen. Really beautiful."

And he hurried up the ladder with Buddy following right behind him.

THE LAST FIRE TRUCK left at the exact moment when Edith and Dodge were supposed to be walking up the white carpet from the house. Instead, the firemen had trampled the carpet, and their equipment had pretty much destroyed every flower and streamer that had been so carefully fastened along the fence.

The good news was Gavin had been freed from the hay bin after being locked up for more than an hour. He hadn't been scared because the box was so old he had a lot of places to see out and Colt, his two brothers, along with Joey and Buddy had entertained him. The country band that Travis hired for the reception had played happy cowboy songs, and the guests had sung along.

The bad news was Gavin still twitched.

Dodge and Edith decided to postpone the actual wedding for a few hours and have the reception first, which gave Colt time to talk to Helen.

"You stayed," Colt said when he finally saw Helen again. His shirt was dirty from crawling around on the floor of the loft. He had hay stuck to his clothes and in his hair. He needed a bath in the worst way, but he couldn't afford to give up this time with Helen.

"I promised Dodge."

"Since when?"

"Since the other night when he stopped me from going into Tater's stall."

Colt had just gotten over his nervous stomach and she'd gone and made it nervous all over again. Tater had been prickly for three days running. He couldn't even get near him, let alone enter his stall. He was better now that the medicine was taking effect but that horse was still a bit spooked.

"Is that when he wrenched his arm?"

"Yes. It was all my fault. I insisted on going into the stall. If it wasn't for your father, there's no telling what could have happened."

"Dodge has a sixth sense."

She gave him a sheepish look. "Aren't you angry with me?"

Colt could no more be angry with her than he could be angry at Gavin. They had both come through their ordeals unscathed and that was enough for him.

"What good would that do?"

"Don't you want to tell me *I told you so?*"

"Tater already did. Other than that, I'm so very glad you're here."

He was fishing now, fishing for something that told him she was willing to work things out.

"I told you, I missed the boys."

He laughed out loud, and she joined in on the laughter. "How could you possibly miss my boys? They make more smoke than wet firewood."

"That's why I love 'em. You never know what they're going to do next. Is Gavin all right?"

"He's fine. It's his dad who's worse for wear."

"You look great to me."

And there it was…her smile. He'd walk a desert to see that smile.

"Not really. I look awful, but you look beautiful, or did I tell you that already?'

"A girl can never hear it too often."

"Then stick around, babe, and I'll tell you every single day for the rest of your life."

"Is that a promise?"

That was all the lead-in Colt needed. He took her in his arms and kissed her, not caring who was watching or what they were saying. He kissed her hard and heavy, as if he'd been thirsty for her lips on his.

When he finally had his fill, he stopped and everyone watching applauded, letting out catcalls and hoots. Helen blushed so red her face almost matched her hair color. He figured he must have looked like a beet himself, but he wasn't about to pay it no mind at all. That kiss had been enough to make a preacher blush and he was proud of it.

Buddy, Gavin and Joey came rushing up to them, each boy talking at the same time.

"You've got to show her, Daddy. I can't stop itching," Gavin said.

"Dad, you need to take her now. Please. Come on, Dad," Buddy insisted.

Soon the guests got in on the demands, as well. "Do it, man!"

"Drive her over there!"

"Show her what you've done!"

"What are they talking about, Colt?" Helen asked, looking confused. "Is it your processing plant? I know you've started it and it's okay. I've made peace with your decision. We can add an arena out behind your house like you suggested. That should work just fine."

It was time. Wedding or no wedding, he had to show her what he'd done.

"Come with me, sweetheart. I've got something to show you."

WHEN COLT PARKED his SUV in front of the old M & M Riding School, Helen braced herself. Sure she'd come to terms with what he was doing, but she felt apprehensive about seeing the destruction.

Also, ever since her night with Tater she'd been having contractions and she was having one as they pulled up to the school. Dr. Guru had examined her and said they were nothing to worry about, but considering she still had two more weeks to go until her due date, Helen was very worried. The doctor had told her to go to the hospital if they intensified, and Helen was now considering what *intensified* actually meant. Ever since Gavin had been freed from the hay bin, they'd gotten worse. Not quite bad enough to be rushed to the hospital…yet. She was hoping they were simply a false alarm kind of thing. Especially since almost every guest had followed them over from the Granger ranch, including Mush and Suzie.

She would have liked it much better if she, Colt and the boys had been able to drive over by themselves, but then living in Briggs was like that. For better or worse everyone wanted to be in on the latest gossip, scandals and good news.

Colt came around and helped her out of the SUV, took her hand and led her past the row of Rocky Mountain maple trees that hadn't quite lost all their leaves yet. Once past the trees she immediately noticed the old house was still standing. Funny thing was, it didn't look anything like the last time she'd seen it. Instead the house appeared to have been freshly painted, and the front porch had been fixed. And there was a new roof and the bright red front door was partially open, as if someone lived there.

"Colt, what is all this?"

"It's ours, babe. Yours and mine. We own it now."

"But what about the other ranchers and the storage plant? Isn't that what you've been doing out here?"

He tilted his head and gave her a smile. "That's what I was trying to tell you the other night at the tavern."

"But I wouldn't listen."

His smile broadened as he took her hand. She was so full of love for him she couldn't contain herself and her eyes watered. He noticed and gladly gave her his handkerchief.

"We did it," Buddy said, excitement bubbling in his voice.

Colt's boys were dancing all around her, along with Scout, who wore a blue dress and tan grown-up cowgirl boots. Helen thought she liked her pink ones better.

"We all did it. Nearly everybody we know. Daddy said

it had to be ready when Gramps and Edith got married. And today they're getting married. We did it!" Gavin said, opening his arms and twirling around.

"Do you like it?" Joey asked. "We fixed it all up real pretty so you could be our other mother. We have one up in heaven, but we need one down here, too. Our mama up in heaven can't scold us and tell us to be good or make us hot chocolate. But you can."

Helen leaned over and gave him a kiss on top of his head. She wanted to kiss his little face, but she couldn't reach it. Her contracting belly got in the way. Tears tumbled down her cheeks and she wiped them with Colt's hankie.

"I'd love to be your other mama, if it's okay with Gavin and Buddy."

"Yes! Yes! Yes!" all three boys shouted, giving her great big hugs.

"Yay!" Scout cheered. "I have a new auntie!"

And once again, everyone clapped and cheered.

When the kids' excitement died down, Colt said, "She hasn't even seen the whole place yet. Let's complete the tour."

This time Gavin took her hand. "Well, come on and hurry up. It's pretty. I even have my own room. We already moved in, and Dodge and Edith are moving into our house as soon as they get back from Texas for their honeymoon."

"Texas? Why Texas?"

"Didn't Milo tell you?" Buddy asked, but he didn't wait for her reply. "He gave Gramps his winning trip to the ranch on that cooking show. Amanda couldn't go because of school and Milo doesn't want to go anywhere without Amanda. They're in love."

"He never told me a thing." She turned to Colt. "Or was that the big news he wanted to share at Belly Up?"

"I think so," Colt said, making a face then nodding.

"How'd you keep all those secrets for so long, Gavin?" Helen asked.

"Easy. You were never here, but, oh boy, once I saw you today, it was impossible!" He threw his hands up in the air.

She looked over at Colt and he took her other hand, and as he did, another contraction rocked her and this time she held her breath. This one really hurt, but Helen still would not believe it was her time. She really didn't want to disrupt Edith's wedding any more than it had been already.

"It's all for you, sweetheart. It's because of you that I finally got my head on straight," Colt told her as he led her inside the house, which was nearly finished, except for paint and furniture.

"We brought over our beds and our clothes and the kids' toys, but everything else we either gave away or stored in the barn."

Travis, who had been trailing behind them, explained the details of the house and the upgrades he'd made. Then everyone went out to the school and had a tour of the renovated classrooms. There were only three that Helen planned on using for lectures mostly.

When they walked out to the covered arena, Helen fell in love with the place all over again. It was meticulously restored and could now easily hold competitions with the added seating on the right and left sides.

As she turned to tell Colt how much she loved him and everything she'd seen, she felt something run down her leg. In that instant, a crushing pain rocked her hard and she clutched Colt's arm so tight she could feel his entire body tense.

"What's wrong?" he said, a frightened look crossing his face.

"My water broke."

"Let's get you to the hospital."

She instinctively knew that wasn't possible. This baby was coming out *now.* "There isn't time."

Buddy came over. "What's wrong with Helen, Dad? I'm scared."

"The baby's coming. Don't be scared. Everything's going to be fine. I promise." His face reflected assurance and confidence. It gave Helen exactly what she needed to brave out the contractions.

"Are you sure?" Gavin asked as he came up behind Colt.

Colt gathered his sons in front of him. "You boys have my word, so don't be scared or worry."

Helen looked down at her new sons. "Don't you guys stress about a thing. I'm going to be just—"

But the pain gripped her so strong she couldn't finish her sentence.

Edith hurried over without having to be asked. Like Dodge, she had that sixth sense about people, and at that moment, Helen couldn't think of another person in the entire world she'd rather have to help deliver this baby more than Edith Abernathy, The Perfect Nurse.

Edith turned to Colt. "Fetch Kendra and Maggie's sister, Kitty. Them girls are good at babies." Then she wrapped her white fringed shawl around Helen's shoulders and said, "Come on, sweetie. Let's get you someplace private."

And as soon as Helen saw the shawl up close she

knew it was the exact shawl from the picture of the nude in Belly Up.

"It's you," Helen told Edith. "You're the woman on the chaise lounge."

"Certainly it's me. Anybody can see the resemblance if they looked at her face instead of her body. I was one hot tamale in those days. Still am, according to Dodge."

Helen giggled. "He knows?"

"Only man in this whole town who knew it was me. I had to marry him after that just to keep him from spreading it around. Now let's you and me go have ourselves a baby."

Epilogue

Helen eased Tater into a faster canter, making their usual tight circle in front of the course. The buzzer sounded and Helen drew her first weapon, leaned forward in the saddle, and Tater took off at lightning speed for the semicircle of five red balloons. At once, Helen aimed her .45, clicked back the rough hammer, pulled the trigger and popped the first balloon, then the second, third, fourth and fifth. She quickly holstered her gun and drew the second firearm, all the while guiding Tater around the red barrel at the far end of the course. She took aim once again and popped each of the five remaining white balloons on the run down as she and Tater raced straight to the end of the course. Holstering her second gun, totally in sync with her horse, totally in tune with the power of the event, Helen knew she'd finally won the championship.

Moments later her winning score came up on the huge digital board at the end of the arena.

The crowd cheered as the announcer yelled his "woo-hoo" into the microphone. Then he gave the audience her official time and Helen knew for certain she was the national champion. This win came with a payout worth over one hundred thousand dollars, and the trophy buckle she coveted.

"We did it, boy," she said all full of smiles and happiness as she stroked Tater's neck then patted his hindquarters. She pulled out her earplugs then waved to the crowd. The cheers got louder and echoed off the metal stands that surrounded the arena. Tater seemed to know they'd won and trotted out of the arena with his head held high.

Tater slowed to an easy canter as they made their way through the metal gate. Then, in the next instant, a female reporter rode up beside her for an interview from the local paper.

"Helen Granger, how does it feel to win the national championship?"

"It feels great, thanks. But I couldn't have done it without my family cheering me on."

"We've heard a lot about them recently, how they're with you during all the events, and especially about your son Buddy, who seems to be following in your footsteps."

"It's been a joy to watch him do so well. He works hard at the sport, and I'm sure that one day he'll be sitting where I am right now."

Helen felt certain Buddy would one day win his share of championships.

"There's been some rumors that this is the end of the road for you. That you won't be going on to try for the world championship. Is that true?"

Helen spotted Colt, the boys and their sweet toddler, Loran, waving like mad up in the stands. "Absolutely. It was a dream of mine to win just one title and my family supported me while I've won several. It's been a fabulous run, but now I want to focus my attention on my family and my riding school."

"With four children and a riding school to run, it's hard to imagine all that you've accomplished this past year. Any insight you want to give us on how you did it?"

"Simple. I'm married to the best cowboy a cowgirl could ever ask for. He's been there for me through it all, and I'm truly blessed to have him by my side."

The reporter looked over at Helen's family. "You have a beautiful family. You must be very proud."

Helen tugged at her lapis lazuli necklace as she gazed up at Colt, who wore a warm grin as he held little Loran in his right arm, while the boys stood on their seats waving.

He mouthed, "I love you," just as Loran knocked his hat off his head. Colt went to grab it but it got away from him and rolled right into the arena. Joey climbed over the gate to retrieve it, followed closely by Gavin and Buddy.

Two wranglers came running out after them, which caused the boys to dart out of their reach. The audience must have thought they were part of the show and cheered for the boys. The announcer played an old cowboy song that only enhanced the ensuing chaos. The reporter put her microphone down and sat there watching. Colt called for his boys to let the hat go and come on back to their seats, but the boys acted as if they couldn't hear him.

Finally, Buddy picked up the rolling hat, and held it up for his dad to see. Then he bowed to the audience as if he'd just accomplished a major task.

The next rider and the audience applauded as the Granger boys climbed back over the railing to get to their seats.

Colt looked over at Helen and shrugged. Helen smiled and shrugged back.

Then Helen looked at the reporter and said, "Without a doubt, they're the best thing that ever happened to me."

* * * * *

COMING NEXT MONTH FROM

HARLEQUIN

American Romance

Available April 1, 2014

#1493 SWEET CALLAHAN HOMECOMING
Callahan Cowboys
by Tina Leonard

Xav Phillips has loved free-spirited Ashlyn Callahan from afar for years, and when he finds out she's had his children—quadruplets!—in secret, he's determined to bring her and his new family home. *Don't miss the exciting finale of the Callahan Cowboys series!*

#1494 IN A COWBOY'S ARMS
Hitting Rocks Cowboys
by Rebecca Winters

After her father's death, Sadie Corkin returns to her Montana ranch home—and Jarod Bannock, the love of her life. Will he forgive her for running away on the eve of their wedding all those years ago?

#1495 TEXAS DAD
Fatherhood
by Roz Denny Fox

He's a father, a rancher, a widower—and Mack Bannerman's daughter wants to find him a wife. Little does she know that the woman she's got in mind, New York photographer JJ Walker, has a past with her Texas dad!

#1496 A COWBOY'S ANGEL
by Pamela Britton

Mariah Stewart is an animal-rights activist, and she's nothing but trouble for race-horse owner Zach Johnson—in more ways than one! Because he can't seem to remember she's the enemy....

———

YOU CAN FIND MORE INFORMATION ON UPCOMING HARLEQUIN® TITLES, FREE EXCERPTS AND MORE AT WWW.HARLEQUIN.COM.

HARCNM0314

REQUEST YOUR FREE BOOKS!
2 FREE NOVELS PLUS 2 FREE GIFTS!

⊕ HARLEQUIN®

American ★ Romance®

LOVE, HOME & HAPPINESS

YES! Please send me 2 FREE Harlequin® American Romance® novels and my 2 FREE gifts (gifts are worth about $10). After receiving them, if I don't wish to receive any more books, I can return the shipping statement marked "cancel." If I don't cancel, I will receive 4 brand-new novels every month and be billed just $4.74 per book in the U.S. or $5.24 per book in Canada. That's a savings of at least 14% off the cover price! It's quite a bargain! Shipping and handling is just 50¢ per book in the U.S. and 75¢ per book in Canada.* I understand that accepting the 2 free books and gifts places me under no obligation to buy anything. I can always return a shipment and cancel at any time. Even if I never buy another book, the two free books and gifts are mine to keep forever.

154/354 HDN F4YN

Name	(PLEASE PRINT)

Address	Apt. #

City	State/Prov.	Zip/Postal Code

Signature (if under 18, a parent or guardian must sign)

Mail to the **Harlequin® Reader Service:**
IN U.S.A.: P.O. Box 1867, Buffalo, NY 14240-1867
IN CANADA: P.O. Box 609, Fort Erie, Ontario L2A 5X3

Want to try two free books from another line?
Call 1-800-873-8635 or visit www.ReaderService.com.

* Terms and prices subject to change without notice. Prices do not include applicable taxes. Sales tax applicable in N.Y. Canadian residents will be charged applicable taxes. Offer not valid in Quebec. This offer is limited to one order per household. Not valid for current subscribers to Harlequin American Romance books. All orders subject to credit approval. Credit or debit balances in a customer's account(s) may be offset by any other outstanding balance owed by or to the customer. Please allow 4 to 6 weeks for delivery. Offer available while quantities last.

Your Privacy—The Harlequin® Reader Service is committed to protecting your privacy. Our Privacy Policy is available online at www.ReaderService.com or upon request from the Harlequin Reader Service.

We make a portion of our mailing list available to reputable third parties that offer products we believe may interest you. If you prefer that we not exchange your name with third parties, or if you wish to clarify or modify your communication preferences, please visit us at www.ReaderService.com/consumerchoice or write to us at Harlequin Reader Service Preference Service, P.O. Box 9062, Buffalo, NY 14269. Include your complete name and address.

HAR13R

SPECIAL EXCERPT FROM

H HARLEQUIN®

American Romance®

Read on for a sneak peek at
SWEET CALLAHAN HOMECOMING *by* USA TODAY
bestselling author Tina Leonard

*Xav Phillips has pined after Ashlyn Callahan—the wiliest
and most footloose of all the Callahan siblings—for years.
But it seems* she *may have caught* him!

"These are your babies?"

She nodded, and he suddenly felt dizzy. The woman he
loved was a mother, and somehow she'd had four children.
This perfect four of a kind was hers.

It wasn't possible. He felt weak all over, weak-kneed in
a way he'd never been, his heart splintering like shattered
glass.

"Damn, Ash, your family… You haven't told them."

"No, I haven't."

A horrible realization sank into him, painful and searing.
"Who's the father?"

She frowned. "A dumb, ornery cowboy."

"That doesn't sound like you. You wouldn't fall for a
dumb, ornery cowboy."

"Yes, I would," Ash said. "I would, and I did."

He looked at the tiny bundles of sweetness in their bas-
sinets. Two girls and two boys, he presumed, because each
bassinet had colored blankets—two pink, two blue. Two of
each. He felt sad, sick, really, that the woman he adored
had found someone else in the nine months she'd been

gone. He felt a little betrayed, sure that the two of them had shared something, although neither of them had ever tried to quantify exactly what that was. "He really is dumb, if he's not here taking care of you," Xav said, and it had to be the truth or she wouldn't be living with the woman with the wicked swing, who'd tried to crush his cranium. "Ash, I'll marry you, and take care of you and your children," he said suddenly, realizing how he could finally catch the woman of his dreams without even appearing to be the lovestruck schmuck that he was.

If anyone was father material, it was he.

Don't miss the final book in
Tina Leonard's
CALLAHAN COWBOYS *miniseries!*

An Enduring Love

When tragedy brings Sadie home to Montana horse country, Jarod knows he has only one chance to make things right. There's unfinished business between them, including what really happened that fateful night. And now there's a more immediate threat to their happiness: an enemy who wants Sadie's ranch to create a cattle empire. Can Jarod find a way to stay true to his heritage and trust in the love that is his destiny?

Look for

In a Cowboy's Arms,

the first title in the new
Hitting Rocks Cowboys miniseries

by REBECCA WINTERS

from Harlequin® American Romance®.

Available wherever books and ebooks are sold.

Love the Harlequin book you just read?

Your opinion matters.

Review this book on your favorite book site, review site, blog or your own social media properties and share your opinion with other readers!